WHITE HEAT

A Heat of Love Novella

BY LETA BLAKE

An Original Publication from Leta Blake Books

White Heat
Written and published by Leta Blake
Cover by Dar Albert
Formatted by BB eBooks

First Print Edition, 2021
ISBN: 978-1-626226-55-5

'90s Coming of Age Series
Pictures of You
You Are Not Me

Winter Holidays

North's Pole

The Mr. Christmas Series
Mr. Frosty Pants
Mr. Naughty List
Mr. Jingle Bells

A Boy for All Seasons
My December Daddy

Fantasy

Any Given Lifetime

Re-imagined Fairy Tales

Flight
Levity

Paranormal & Shifters

Angel Undone
Omega Mine

Horror

Raise Up Heart

Omegaverse

Heat of Love Series
Slow Heat
Alpha Heat
Slow Birth
Bitter Heat

For Sale Series
Heat for Sale
Bully for Sale

Audiobooks
letablake.com/audiobooks

Discover more about the author online

Leta Blake
letablake.com

Acknowledgments

Thank you to the following people: Mom and Dad, Brian and Cecily. All the wonderful members of my Patreon who inspire, support, and advise me. Keira Andrews for constant cheerleading and developmental edits. Sue Laybourn for the amazing editing work. Willow for the fantastic copyedits and proofing. Melissa for the secondary proofing. Dar Albert for the gorgeous cover. And thank you to my readers who make it writing stories like this so worthwhile.

Forbidden love conquers all

In an ancient journal dating from the early years following the Great Death when the world was divided into kingdoms known as Lineages, Vale Aman uncovers a tale of forbidden love and boundless devotion.

Sian Maxima, the heir to a great Lineage, wants to marry his childhood sweetheart, Avila Rossi. But their love is outlawed. After a secret, desperate tryst is discovered, Avila alone will be punished for their transgressions.

Only Sian can save him.

Within the journal's pages, Vale finds a story to inspire and strengthen him while he waits to find an equally great love of his own.

White Heat is a standalone prequel to the book *Slow Heat* in Leta Blake's *Heat of Love* universe. It's set against a faux-historical backdrop in a post-apocalyptic world containing omegaverse tropes such as knotting, mpreg, and heats.

CHAPTER ONE

"In the Old World, before the Great Death, many considered there to be two main expressions of human form—male and female. In the destruction after the Great Death, when all human females were lost, our generous wolf-god moved to aid humankind.

Hating to see the suffering of men left alone in the world, his compassionate love created the three forms of man: alpha—the inseminator, omega—the womb-carrier, and beta—the infertile."

—Excerpt from *Historical Ages of Wolf* by
Eretan Maden

Definition of *Érosgápe*: an alpha or omega's biologically and spiritually determined mate

Example of *Érosgápe* **in a sentence**: some alphas and omegas are not just contracted mates, but are *Érosgápe*, bound deeply by spirit and flesh.

Origin and Etymology of *Érosgápe*: Old World Greek, literally sexual love (*erōs*) and spiritual love (*agapē*) combined.

First Known Use: Year 32 of Wolf

Year 654 of Wolf

"IN THE EARLY years after the Great Death, wolf-god blessed us with omegas to replace the lost human women," Professor Chuez said as he paced in front of the large, empty whiteboard. "Humanity had been utterly decimated. Every child an omega could conceive and bear alive was needed to grow the population, and every life was required to move us out of the Dark Ages. Murder was beyond taboo, even more so than it is today. It was a very old-fashioned time. Omegas were treated as commodities more than as men, and sex and fertility were strictly controlled."

Vale sat in his hard chair, surrounded by his fellow omega students. He fought a smirk at Professor Chuez's words. As if reproduction wasn't strictly controlled *now*.

Omegas were still sent away to schools like Mont Juror as teens to "learn their place in the world." They were still put on heat suppressants at puberty to control the timing of their first heat. And, even now, if they weren't lucky enough to find their *Érosgápe*, omegas were treated as commodities for alphas to bid on or tussle over, whether the omegas liked it or not.

An omega's consent was ostensibly required these days to be taken, bred, or contracted with, but what was consent, really, when heats existed? Especially since access to heat suppressants was, for all intents and purposes, revoked after an omega reached majority, graduated, and was of legal childbearing age. The Holy Church of Wolf and the associated government still had clear priorities, and, to them, human rights and sexual ethics mattered much less than aggressive population growth.

Rolling his eyes, Vale thought bitterly: *Gotta make those babies!*

As bad as things often were for omegas now, Vale could concede that, in the beginning years of wolf, things had been much, much worse. In those days, his kind had been at the mercy of the Lineages. Each Lineage had their own distinct laws based on their Lineage Leader's interpretation of the Holy Book of Wolf. Some Lineages were strict, some were stricter. Few were lenient and even those that were considered loose by the standards of the time held limited ideas about omegas' consent.

Vale had learned all about these dark days in Early Post-Old World History last year.

That had been when he'd met Henry, too. Or Mr. Marks, he should say.

The handsome librarian had helped him with his research for his term paper and had become the object of Vale's secret fantasies. It was odd that an alpha was allowed on campus, and even odder that he was so patient, calm, and gentle. Not like most alphas of Vale's acquaintance, at all.

Rumor had it that Henry—Mr. Marks—had suffered an accident in his youth that had left him less alpha than he should've been. Whatever that meant. But as far as Vale could tell, he was as attractive as any man could hope to be. And wasn't there something romantic in his sad, lonely state? In the softness of his eyes as he pored over pages in the stately old library?

Vale certainly thought so. These days he thought of little else.

"Mr. Aman, if you refuse to pay attention to my lectures, I'll happily give you a zero for attendance again. A body in a chair is meaningless when your mind is elsewhere."

Vale jerked his attention back to Professor Chuez and murmured an apology. He struggled to keep his focus as the lecture on the Historical Restrictions on Omega Sexual Practices continued. It should have been fascinating, but Professor Chuez made it as dry as an old bone. Vale was glad when the bell rang.

"Don't forget!" Professor Chuez called as everyone gathered their things and prepared to leave. "Your term papers will be due by the end of the semester. Start your research now. I expect cohesive arguments with excellent primary sources from each of you. Seek help from Mr. Marks if you have trouble."

Vale stood, hefting his backpack onto his shoulders. His heart had leapt at the name, and he closed his eyes, taking a deep breath to calm himself. It was as if, just by hearing Mr. Marks's name uttered, he could smell the alpha's sandalwood cologne and see his subtle smile.

"Want to head back to the dorm, get changed, and then go down to the river for a swim?" Jordy asked as they stepped out from the stuffy hallway lined with equally stuffy classrooms and into the bright light of the courtyard. "We only have a few more days until the season will start to change, and then no more swimming until spring."

"You go without me," Vale said, his gaze already on the spire set atop the library. "I need to get a head start on this term paper. Professor Chuez has it in for me ever since he caught me writing that silly poem."

"He really does hate you," Jordy agreed, stroking his tight black curls, and lifting his face to the sky. "I mean, it was a *very* insulting poem."

Vale shrugged. If Professor Chuez wanted him to write flattering things about him, then he should be less boring, and less of a blowhard, too.

"I'll see if Yonder wants to go. He's usually game."

It was true Yonder was game for almost anything, and Vale hoped he wouldn't get Jordy into trouble by sneaking some liquor or other contraband out to the river.

After parting ways, Vale's heart started to flutter as he walked up to the library's shaded portico and pulled open the weather-worn oaken door. He hoped his face didn't look as flushed as it felt.

Henry was working today, like every day, behind a big circular desk installed beneath the massive domed ceiling in the middle of the main floor of the library. Vale swallowed hard, wiping his sweaty palms on his pants. Henry wore a blue sweater vest over a long-sleeved white shirt, and his dark beard had been oiled neatly. As always, his thick eyebrows gave his pale face an appealing drama that had caught Vale's eye from the start. Today, though, he looked a little sleepy, as he sorted through a pile of books.

"Hi," Vale said. His pulse throbbed in his ears as Henry turned those smart gray eyes onto him. "Um, I've got a term paper."

Henry smiled and came closer, leaning his elbows on the counter. "Chuez's class, right?"

"Yes."

Henry tilted his head with a soft smile. "Do you have a thesis yet?"

"No, not really."

Henry's chuckle, amused and fond, buzzed like electric arousal up Vale's spine. His asshole grew damp with slick. He hoped Henry didn't scent it. Struggling to get his young libido under control, Vale peered hopefully at Henry. Surely he'd have to help him, right? It was his job, like Professor Chuez said.

Henry turned to the stack of books he'd been sorting before. "I can't help you find books for a thesis that doesn't exist. So come back when you've got a general direction at least."

"Wait…" Vale licked his lips. "Please. Do you have anything to help me? Maybe something unusual? A source no one else has used yet? I really need to impress Chuez."

"What happens if you don't?"

Vale swallowed. "I'll have to hear about it from my pater and maybe even my father if the grade is bad enough."

"Mm." Henry regarded him for another moment.

"Please, Mr. Marks. I'm desperate."

Tutting, Henry capitulated. "All right, I might have something. If you're willing to think outside the box."

"I'm always outside the box," Vale enthused, stepping closer. A buzz started up inside him, and he hoped he didn't leak more. It would be so humiliating if Henry realized how much Vale wanted him. "What is it?"

Henry straightened to his full height and put more distance between them. "Most omegas do their thesis on *Érosgápe* bonds…"

Of course they did. *Érosgápe* bonds represented the greatest love possible, and every omega lived in hope of finding one. An omega's future was all too terrifying, uncertain, and potentially grim if they didn't find their one true mate. Sadly, only about a third of the population did.

"But you like things with drama and romance to them, don't you, Vale?"

Henry knew enough of his reading habits, and

Vale had shown him some of his poetry in the past. None that he'd written about Henry, of course—he wasn't that big of a fool—but rather nature poems, dramatic ones about storms, thunder, and rain. "I do."

Henry smiled. "I know just the thing then. How would you like to write your paper about the strict rules placed on omegas and their sexual expression during the oppressive years of wolf—"

That was the assignment, so he nodded.

"—but unlike the other students, you'll focus on how sexuality and heat were handled in love relationships where there was no *Érosgápe* connection."

"No *Érosgápe* bond?" Was Henry saying what Vale thought he was saying? His heart swelled with hope.

Henry said, "Indeed. There's more than one way to get a happy ending in life."

Vale licked his lips. Was Henry admitting to an interest in Vale, too?

Unlikely, but if Henry believed there could be a love worth having outside of an *Érosgápe* bond then it was at least a start. While Vale wasn't sure he was in love with Henry, per se, there was no doubt he *could* be, and if Vale never found his destiny, then perhaps Henry would still be around, and maybe

Henry would want to try?

Ridiculous. Adolescent romantic dreams. He *knew* this, and yet he remained enamored with Henry's eyes, smile, scent, hands, and the way he so often acted as if Vale was worth talking to.

"You've convinced me," Vale said.

"Great. There's a particular book I've never shared with students because it's too special. But I trust you with it, Vale."

His cheeks grew hot. "Thank you."

"Of course. It'll get you started in the right direction. You'll need a few more books, but as a personal history goes, this ticks all the boxes."

"I'll be the first student you've shown this book to?" Vale asked.

"That's right." Henry smiled. "Come on. This way."

Henry guided Vale deep into the stacks of books, the scent of them mixing pleasantly with Henry's sandalwood cologne. Leading him to a door that read *Reserved Room*, he pulled out a keyring and unlocked it. "You wait in here." He gestured Vale over the threshold. "I'll bring the book to you."

Inside, the room was quite large. It held nine long empty tables with chairs alongside each, all carved from the pale-yellow wood that had been popular several generations before. It'd been excessively used in doctors' offices and schools because it'd been cheap to buy but pleasant to look at. Vale took a seat at the second table back and waited for Henry to return.

The room was quiet, almost entirely silent except for the repetitive song of a cricket trapped somewhere. Dust motes seemed to dance in the sunlight from the vast windows lining one side. What did it mean that Henry had brought him here? There was an intimacy to this situation that he'd never dared to hope for. His heart wanted to believe this was about so much more than simply allowing Vale to look at a book from the *Reserved* collection, but deep down he knew better.

"Here we are," Henry said in his usual hushed voice, coming back through the door with a white box in his hands.

"What's this?" Vale asked, as Henry pulled a cloth-wrapped bundle out of the box and laid it on the table.

"This," he said, taking the seat next to Vale, "is the most romantic story I've ever read."

Vale felt himself growing hot and slick threatened to leak again. *Was* Henry signaling interest in him? "I—I'm supposed to be researching the history of omega rights."

"Yes, I know. This journal has plenty of that,

too," he said, unwrapping the leather-bound, ancient-looking tome. "It's the diary of a young alpha who, due to the early strictures regarding omegas' heats and sexuality and a lack of leniency around non-*Érosgápe* relationships, nearly lost everything dear to him."

"Oh?" Vale's mouth was dry, and he licked his lips, trying not to read more into this, though he was dying to believe Henry was subtly seducing him.

"There's so much to be learned from this piece of history," Henry went on. "But most academic books focus only on the politics, power dynamics, and violence. This personal journal is a nearly forgotten artifact. I've begun the process of having it issued in a print run for libraries and some select booksellers, but it hasn't been cleared by the priests yet. Perhaps one day. But for now, this is the only copy of this story in existence, and I've never shown it to any student but you."

"Why?" Vale asked.

"Because you're full of poetry, Vale," Henry said, and the fondness in his expression almost melted Vale's heart. "And you'll write poems about this story and the men in it. And I want to read your words, see it through your eyes."

"Yes. I will," Vale vowed. Though he meant he'd write more poems about Henry's handsome face, and gleaming eyes, not about whatever was contained in the dusty old journal.

"Here," Henry said, opening the leather cover; the pages inside were crisp, brown, and old. He flipped ahead a bit. "Begin with this entry. Everything before is just stuff and nonsense."

"Why's that?" He hated jumping into the middle of a story.

"Because Sian was still a kid," Henry explained. Then his eyes crinkled at the sides as he smiled again, as if the book and the men in it were old friends. "He's still a child here, too, in many ways, but he changes quickly as things progress with his Avila. Go on. Read it."

Much to Vale's disappointment, Henry rose and left Vale alone with the book. He sighed, listening to the endless drone of the cricket, wishing that his heart didn't ache with longing for a man who was far too old, and far too forbidden.

Eventually, he turned his attention to the page. If he couldn't have Henry by his side, then he was determined to uncover whatever beauty Henry had found in the diary. He'd have that piece of Henry for himself at least. A part no one else had ever known.

Sian Maxima's Journal
Year 136 of Wolf

I FEAR WRITING the words even here, but I'm so full of joy at finally seeing the man I love again that I can't hold it back any longer. If I don't write of my feelings, I'll burst.

My friend Dama once told me journals are good for keeping secrets, and that's why I have written faithfully in you for all these years. But there's one secret I have never confessed.

His name is Avila.

Avila Rossi of the Rossi Lineage.

I feel faint just thinking of him.

I met him almost eight summers ago at the Meeting of Future Lineages, held annually by the Holy Church of Wolf at the Rossi estate. I was only eleven, and normally I wouldn't have been in attendance at such an important event, but Father was terribly unwell and not expected to live much longer. As I am the only alpha of my father's seed and, therefore, the future Head of Lineage for the Maxima family, the council and my father decided that I should get my feet wet at the meeting.

I was sent along with my guardians—alphas of esteem and power in my family—to listen at the meetings and prepare myself for taking the leadership role that I now finally enjoy. Though, as you well know, journal, I am cosseted on all sides by my council, who can overrule any of my decisions until I'm twenty. Still, I'm proud to finally be acknowledged as Lineage Leader.

But, oh, poor Father. The end of his life was difficult. No doubt he found his end welcome, even if I did not. Aside from the physical pain of his illness, Father had been in despair ever since he'd lost my pater, his *Érosgápe* mate, during the birth of my omega brother, Hollis.

Birth is always dangerous for omegas. They are a miracle from wolf-god without a doubt, however, if I may say so, their bodies seem less robust than they should be for their role. But, dear journal, never say I questioned wolf-god's wisdom! If only because I don't want to end up eternally punished for blasphemy.

But I digress.

Avila.

Avila. Avila. *Avila.*

No, he's not my *Érosgápe*, dear journal, but I don't care. He couldn't be more perfect and lovely if he was. I swear it on wolf-god's own eye. I am made more of a man, more of an alpha when I even look at him. And isn't that what omegas are for in this world? To elevate an alpha from mediocrity to something greater, if only in their desire to love and be loved by someone so beautiful, so perfect?

I know I sound besotted, bewitched, under the spell of omega persuasion but, again, I don't care. All I know is I love Avila with all my heart and soul. His black eyes gazing into mine make me feel faint. His smile causes my heart to grow wings and soar out of my body. His long dark hair coming loose around his face after he's been out with the other omegas of his age, walking in the fields collecting flowers makes my knees weak. And never mind how I feel when he comes to meet me wreathed in smiles and wearing a white flower crown on his head…

Wolf-god! I nearly swoon!

You must be wondering, oh, journal friend, how I've come to know Avila at all since I've kept him a secret from you. Omegas and alphas being kept separate as they are, it must seem unlikely I could have had access to Avila's company for long enough to know I love him. You imagine it's just a crush, don't you? But it's not. I know Avila well, and that's a story unto itself.

First off, you must understand, Avila is older than me. He's eligible already. He's an available omega who can be claimed at any point by an alpha of proper standing or an *Érosgápe*. They need only negotiate a marriage with the Rossi Lineage Leader, Avila's father, and take him. Which, frankly, fills me with terror because he's so beautiful! How has no alpha seen fit to make him theirs? Perhaps it's because the Rossi are stingy with their omegas. They want to get a good omega rate for each of them, so they price them far out of most alphas' ability to pay.

But I, however, can afford him.

As soon as *I'm* of an eligible age.

Please, wolf-god, be on our side. He only must stay free for another year, and then I can take him as my very own. That day can't come—

OH, JOURNAL, I apologize. I was interrupted by my friend Dama before I could finish telling you about the first time I met Avila. I rambled far too much in my last entry, so I will try to stay focused this time. It's only, when it comes to Avila, my mind spins. I can't keep my thoughts going in any direction that doesn't end with how soon I can be with him. How soon I can touch him. Hold him. Make him mine.

But back to how we met.

The first year I was taken to the Meeting of Future Lineages, being so far underage, my guardians didn't think a thing of sending me off to run wild on the Rossi estate while they talked between meetings. They thought it was a good way for me to burn off energy. And it was. I raced up the hills, into the forests, and climbed on stones by the river.

Left to my own devices for the full month of meetings, I learned the estate like the back of my hand, often not even bothering to return for the afternoon sessions, because, as I was just a boy, my thoughts weren't needed.

Which finally leads me to the day that started it all, the glorious day I met Avila.

I was eleven, as I said, and boisterous. That day I was wading in the shallows of the river that flows across the Rossi estate, playing at catching fish with my bare hands, when a boy dressed entirely in white—the color preferred by the omegas of the Rossi household—slipped down to the edge of the bank and watched me.

I was immediately struck by his beauty. He had long hair, and unlike most of the omegas at my own estate, no touch of color on his lips—forbidden by the Rossi for being too alluring. My father's omegas wore kohl around their eyes and red gloss on their lips, and sparkling jewelry and colorful, revealing clothing, all in the hope of catching his eye.

In comparison, Avila appeared like a pure, innocent angel, complete with a plain silver barrette to hold the hair away from his face. He moved like a deer, all grace and long limbs, as he climbed over the rocks by the riverside to finally stand glowing in the sun. He watched me with an open, friendly expression. I didn't detect even an ounce of the smug amusement I often saw in older boys when they were met with my childish antics.

"No luck?" Avila asked, as I tried to show off for him, diving in after another fish, and coming up empty-handed.

I shook the water off my arms as I trudged through the shallows toward the bank. My trousers were soaked through. "No," I muttered, pushing my wet hair away from my face so I could see him better. "Fish are smarter than me, I guess."

"Not smarter, just fishier." His eyes crinkled with warm amusement. "They have an advantage in the water. Fins and gills."

As he regarded me, tilting his head and giving me a long look from head to toe, I was suddenly very aware of my scrawny, hairless chest. Grabbing my shirt from where it sat baking in the warm sun, I wiped myself off with it before tugging it on. He watched me with a small smile, but there was nothing unkind in it, nothing mocking.

My damp hair stuck to my face, and there was nothing to be done about my wet, clinging trousers.

Acutely aware that I looked a childish mess in front of this beautiful omega boy, anxiety crept into my heart. But I was still the alpha, and I knew what to do.

"I'm Sian." I put out my hand in the manner of an alpha presenting himself to an omega he commanded. He took hold of my fingers, raised them to his lips, and kissed the knuckles with perfect form. My knees wobbled and the touch tore through me like an arrow to my heart. "Who are you?" I demanded.

"Avila of the Rossi Lineage." He kissed my knuckles again, lifting his lashes to peer at me with a mischievous glint. "Pleased to meet you, Sian of the..." He trailed off meaningfully. "I'm sorry, I didn't catch your Lineage." I'd been rude in not giving my family name, and he knew it. My cheeks burned to have it pointed out.

"Sian of the Maxima Lineage." I puffed out my chest. "Alpha." I clarified it because, mid-pubescent as I was, I wasn't sure he knew. To be fair, *no one* had known for sure until just a year earlier when I'd started exhibiting the signs. My father had been quite relieved, all his other sons having been betas until Hollis was born. But while an omega like Hollis was better than a beta for political purposes, he still wasn't good enough to inherit. So thank wolf-god I'd finally presented.

"Obviously you're an alpha," Avila said with a grin. "What kind of well-trained omega is going to be out here alone, fishing with his bare hands, and demanding knuckle kisses from strangers?"

I flushed harder because I was an idiot.

Of course he'd known I was an alpha from the moment I presented my hand—if he hadn't already known, as he'd also pointed out, by my stupidly rambunctious behavior. Omegas, for the most part, were more refined in their pastimes. Or they were trained to be. That was a classic case of chicken or egg, as far as I could tell.

"And what are you doing here?" I asked, like a little emperor, because that was how I was accustomed to behaving at home. I was—*am*—the sole heir and only alpha son of Axis Maxima, after all.

But Avila tsked at me. "Manners, Sian. Even an alpha needs some manners."

I frowned, trying to think of how to rephrase my question in a more polite way, when he answered it anyway.

"The house is too frenzied." A furrow formed between Avila's perfect, black brows. "My omega brethren are excited by the presence of so many available alphas on the estate. They're hoping for an *Érosgápe* match, of course, because that's the most desirable, but also because Father couldn't dispute it." He said it as though his father often disputed possible matches.

As I watched, Avila sat down on a rock by the riverbank, and picked up a small stone. Impressively, he skipped it over the water. "But I grew tired of listening to their dreaming."

"You don't want to meet your *Érosgápe*?" I remained standing over him, arms crossed, legs planted wide, trying to look bigger and stronger than I was.

Avila shrugged before leaning back on his hands, stretching his long legs out in the sunshine, and hitching up his white pants to expose his pale shins and calves. The sun glinted off his long black hair, and his fair face glowed. I felt a little dizzy at the sight. "What would you say, little alpha, if I told you I don't think I ever will meet him? So I don't bother looking anymore."

I crouched down close to him, my wet pants clinging in awkward places, but he had me curious now. What omega didn't want to find an *Érosgápe*? What alpha didn't for that matter? Everyone knew *Érosgápe* love is the best love. "Why won't you look for him?"

"Because he's dead."

I flinched back from the words. "'Dead?' How

do you know?"

Avila stood and moved away from me. His hair swung with his steps, and his sigh drifted over his shoulder, as he headed into the shadows offered by the big trees. I stood too, watching as he sank down on another big rock near the river, but this one shielded from the sun. "You'll think I'm as silly as my brothers do if I tell you."

I rushed to him, unable to tolerate him telling me what I'd think, especially that I'd ever think anything negative about him. I'd already decided Avila was the most perfect and beautiful omega I'd ever met, and I had already decided that would never change. "Tell me anyway," I ordered. "I want to know." Again, I was so spoiled back then, I didn't know any better than to speak to him like that.

Avila didn't seem to mind. He gazed at me like he thought I was sweet, and his smile made my chest feel hot and messy, and my stomach go all tumble-y.

"Well, when you put it like that..." Avila's eyes twinkled before growing more solemn. "When I was younger, perhaps your age, I felt something—" he put a hand to his heart and his expression grew dark. "Here. A kind of severing. As if a part of me I hadn't known was there—a thread of love is how I described it to my pater at the time—was cut away. I knew in that moment he was gone from this earth.

That I would never know him. It hurt." He frowned, and my heart sped up. "Perhaps it hurt less because I never met him? Perhaps that's why I was able to live through the pain?"

"Maybe." I watched him for a moment, the way the shadows of the leaves shifted over his skin and clothes, the way his black eyes caught and held my reflection as he gazed back at me. Then I sat down beside him on the rock, careful to keep my wet pants from touching his pristine form, murmuring, "I'm sorry you lost him."

Avila tilted his head, the light in his eyes sharpening on me. "You believe me? No one ever does."

"Why wouldn't I believe you?" I said with a frown, picking up a small stone and turning it over in my hand. "Why would you lie about a thing like that? It'd be stupid. Of course you're telling the truth."

"Thank you," he said, and my heart tumble-skipped at the softness of his voice. "I appreciate that, little alpha. It's very good of you."

"Well, I'm a good person," I said, tossing the stone into the river, and failing miserably at skipping it. I took up another, tried again, and this time it hopped like a frog three whole times. I crossed my arms over my chest in satisfaction. "I'm gonna be a great alpha, too."

"I bet."

"For real! I am!"

"I know! I believe you!" Avila shot those words at me with the same insistent inflection I'd used, and then he smiled. "You're cute. Do the Maxima know you're out here?"

"They don't care. They say they want me here at the meeting to 'learn' but when they get into the thick of their business, they just want me gone."

Avila was quiet for a moment. "I hear your father is sick."

I winced. "He's not long for this world, Rhineheld says."

"Rhineheld," Avila said with a thoughtful expression. "He's the alpha your father has entrusted with your care and with the decisions for the Lineage until you're of age, right?"

"How do you know that?"

"Omegas are great gossips, you know," he said with another disarming twinkle. "We like to talk."

"Hmmph." I didn't like to think the omegas of the Rossi household were talking about my father or my Lineage. But then again, now I was curious. "What do the omegas from the various Lineages say about me?"

"About you?"

I lifted my chin. "You heard me. Don't stall. I

can take it."

"They think you're a handsome little thing. Bound to make one of our younger brothers, or one of the younger boys of another Lineage, a good *Érosgápe* if they're lucky."

Suddenly certain—I can't explain it, journal, I just knew—I lifted my chin and declared, "*I* won't find an *Érosgápe* either. So then what?"

Avila's lips twitched. "You don't dream of a perfect love? A match like no other?"

"Who needs that? So much bother. So much nonsense."

"Your parents were *Érosgápe*, weren't they?"

"Yes."

Avila studied me for a moment. "Ah, and you don't like what's happened to your father after your pater's death. The way he's declined."

I frowned at him, not liking how he'd deduced so much when I'd given him so little. But Avila could always see through me. "How? Maybe that's true. But I've already decided on my omega."

"Is that right?" Avila laughed then, outright and loud, and my heart thudded with a violence I'd never known before. I didn't know what to make of it, dear journal. I didn't understand then what I was proclaiming. I just knew what I said next was the truth, whether Avila liked it or not.

"That's *right*."

He blinked at me, his long lashes glittering in the sunlight. "I suppose you expect me to ask who now? Let me guess—there's a pretty omega on your estate. Someone not blood-related. A teacher of the younger omegas, perhaps? Oh, I know. Rhineheld's youngest? He's pretty." He tutted. "Although, he's a little bastard, if you ask me. Far too sure of himself. I mean, yes, he has nice eyes, but who doesn't have something nice about them? We all do." He flicked his long hair over his shoulders. "So, which is it? I guessed right with Rhineheld's youngest, didn't I? Is it Miracules?"

"It's you."

Avila went still for a moment and then laughed again, a long laugh, the kind that bent his body over and made him hold his stomach as tears came to his eyes.

I gritted my teeth and waited for it to stop.

When he was wiping the wetness from his lash-es, and no longer tittering so much, I said, "I promise. I will marry you. And you will like it."

He laughed again.

Oh, journal, I must have seemed like such a child. But I meant it then, and I mean it now. I'll mean it forever.

JOURNAL, IT'S BEEN several days, I know, but my advisors have kept me busy.

I still haven't told you all the reasons I hope for Avila to be mine. Skimming back over what I last wrote, I told you about how we first met, and that I knew, immediately, I would have him as my omega.

I'll skip ahead now. There's too much to cover otherwise.

Suffice it to say, over the years, we've spent a lot of time together. As it turned out, Avila enjoyed my company, and each summer during the month-long meeting, he and I met often by the river. We grew to know and like each other more and more as we explored deeper into the hills around the Rossi estate, taking long walks by the riverbed side-by-side. He'd tell me about his various brothers—alpha, beta, and omega—and their challenges dealing with his strict and cruel father, and I'd tell him about the fears I had about becoming Lineage Leader.

When my father finally did die, after years of prolonged decline and suffering, Avila was the only one I trusted to pour out my pain and sadness to. Anyone else would have seen it as weakness. Now, as Lineage Leader, weak is one thing I can never again be. Others will take advantage of any weakness of mine they can find to exploit. Avila, though, would never hurt me. He put his arm around my shoulders and kissed my cheek. That alone was so thrilling that I almost forgot my grief for a moment. He held my hand, too. But he's never touched me more than that.

In all our time together, Avila has never laughed at my problems or my worries or my grief—only at my declarations of love for him, and my determination to marry him.

It was during my fifth year of attendance at the meetings that Avila said to me, not for the first time, "You're so silly, and I'm much too old for you."

"You're three years older. That's not all that many."

"I can't wait for you, though, Sian," he'd countered.

We were again by the river, this time farther upstream, deeper in the forest, and away from any prying eyes. Not that Avila had ever allowed me to do anything that needed to be hidden from anyone's eyes—aside from being with him alone. As I said, sometimes he'd let me hold his hand, but nothing more.

"Why can't you wait for me?" I demanded.

"I have heats to deal with, after all." He cast his eyes down, his voice going soft and sad.

"You do?" I spat the words, outraged. The very idea of another alpha helping him with a heat, of Avila squirming on another man's knot, of him bearing that man's child infuriated me. "I'll handle your heats from now on, then. I can make a knot," I said feverishly, sure I could. An omega on my estate had passed near me when he was just starting to go into heat, and his scent had left me aroused. When I'd hidden in a bush close enough to still suck in his delicious scent, but not where anyone could see me, I'd made myself come and developed a knot at the base of my fist. "Let me do it," I insisted. "I can knot you."

"You're not old enough," Avila said with a horrible, broken-sounding laugh. "Rhineheld and the others won't let you marry me. You're only sixteen. Facts are facts."

I *was* old enough by that point to note Avila hadn't said he wouldn't marry me, or that he didn't want to, only that my advisors wouldn't allow it. And he was right on that count. But I knew I could convince them once I was at my majority. If only Avila could wait…

But heats waited for no man. Not even an arrogant little alpha like me.

Heart on fire, stomach churning, I asked, "Who's your father going to match you to then?" I'd find the man and make it very clear it wasn't in his interests to knot Avila, or impregnate him, and then I'd make it even more clear to Avila's father that *I* would be the best man for the job. I wasn't above using the Maxima Lineage's power for this. Nothing mattered more to me. Avila would be my omega, the pater of my children. I'd decided it. So it would happen. "Who will it be? Tell me."

Avila frowned and said slowly, almost reluctantly, "I don't know. Father might not."

"Might not what?"

"He might not match me. For my heat."

"Absurd." All omegas on my estate were matched for their heats, and children were born haphazardly if the heat matches didn't last. It was different, of course, for omegas of prestigious backgrounds, but all families matched their sons off, well before their first heat arrived, to avoid the emotional trauma associated with an unserviced heat. "No alpha father wants to see his omega sons suffer," I said. "He'll *have* to match you temporarily or marry you off. It might as well be me."

"Well, he doesn't have to see the suffering, does he?" Avila said, face pale. He didn't meet my eyes, gazing off into the trees.

My blood ran cold. "What do you mean?"

As I said, we were sitting by the river that day,

the forested hills behind us stretching into the distance. I could hear the creak of the wood as the wind shifted through the trees. Suddenly, Avila turned and stared at the path leading up into the woods. Finally, he stood and took my hand. "Come with me. I'll show you something."

The forest was dense, the footpath cluttered with roots and rogue white flowers. The climb left me huffing, but at the end of the trail there was a circle of five small houses. Well, "houses" is a strong word. More like huts. Avila led me into one of them. It was dark inside, windowless.

"What's this place?" I asked.

"It's a heat house."

I grimaced. "A heat house? What alpha would want to couple for the full period of a heat in here? There aren't even planks on the floor." It was just packed earth beneath my feet. The heat houses on the Maxima estate were plush, decadent even, with beds and soft pillows to allow mating on every surface, for as long as it took for the heat to pass.

"They don't."

"What are you saying?" I turned to Avila wide-eyed. My heart thrashed in my chest. My lungs ached.

"These are the heat houses for the unmarried omegas. Father doesn't allow for unsanctified matches. He believes it's against wolf-god's wishes for us to breed without the blessing of the priests."

My head spun. The implications of what Avila was telling me were beyond horrible. "Then why not marry you off before—"

Avila shook his head. "Father wants to make perfect matches. It's not about the price. Not like many think. He wants his Lineage to be refined. No low-brow connections. He'd rather we die unbred than—"

"That is utterly against wolf-god's maxims!" I shouted. "You're for breeding!"

Avila flinched. "I like to think I'm for something more than that. Loving, perhaps?"

Awash in rage at Avila's father and fear for Avila's future, and also with adoration for him, I flung my arms around his neck. I nuzzled his hair and breathed him in, whispering, "You're for loving, yes, Avila. I love you. I've always loved you."

Avila tugged away from me immediately, gasping at my presumption in embracing him. "Don't," he whispered. "If someone saw—" He looked around the dark heat house, his eyes wide. The narrow door looked out to an empty circle of grass. His shoulders sank with relief. "No one is here. My omega brothers are all between heats now." His lips twisted into a smirk. "This isn't the sort of place people want to visit, is it? So… It's fine. I'm sure no one saw us. It's fine."

He seemed to be reassuring himself more than me.

"Forgive me," I said, taking hold of his long fingers again. "I didn't mean to take liberties. It's just…" My heart beat wildly. "I mean it when I say I love you, and I want to knot you, and marry you, and raise the heirs to my Lineage with you. Why do you think I won't be able to convince your father to let me be the one to handle your heats? To marry you?"

"Because I have a heat very soon, Sian," he murmured, leaning his forehead down to mine. He was still taller. "There's no way. You're too young. Rhineheld and your advisors won't agree, and so long as they don't agree, neither will my father. Your Lineage is too powerful to anger, and—"

"Then your father shouldn't anger me then, should he? If I demand your hand and womb, then he'll have to hold them for me, won't he?"

"Perhaps he will. But that might not be a good thing either." Avila glanced around the hut. "I've spent one heat here," he whispered. "In this hut." He moved to the door and swung it out so that the inside of it was visible in the sunlight. Furrowed scratches lined the wood. "These are my fingernail

34

marks. I screamed. I begged. The lock stayed tight."

"I will never let that happen to you again," I whispered vehemently, rage swelling in my soul.

Avila smiled sadly. "Oh, Sian, you're going to make such a fierce alpha one day, but for now…"

"One day?" I broadened my stance. "I'm fierce now."

"You are," he agreed, and then reached out for my hand again. "Let's go. I don't want to be here before I need to be."

"You'll never be here again."

That, journal, was the first lie I ever told Avila. The first of many, but I didn't know it then.

Avila was right. When I presented my demands to the gathered Lineages, my advisors told me to sit down. Then they stood up and presented at length their arguments against allowing a young man who hadn't even reached the age of majority to connect himself with an omega from any of the Lineages at this time. The need to make a political alliance might yet be ahead, and to waste a precious thing like marriage on a young boy's crush, on a horny alpha's fancy for an omega he'd met in passing— well, it was absurd. Avila's father agreed. My request was denied.

I learned at the next meetings, a year later, that Avila had spent two hideous heats in the huts on the hill.

After he confessed this, he touched my hair, running his fingers through it in absolution as I knelt at his feet and begged him to forgive me for not being born earlier.

He didn't laugh at that.

To be honest, journal, in recent years, my Avila laughs less and less. We both do.

JOURNAL, MY LAST entry grew very dark in subject matter, and I found I couldn't continue on with it. It's been a few days since I wrote, but I'm back again, determined to record my feelings for and commitment to Avila.

I get to see him very soon! I cannot wait!

I'm nineteen now. This is the final year standing between us and my age of majority. When I turn twenty, I'll take the leadership of the Lineage. I'll own my life, my decisions, and my mating after that. At this point, though, even my cock is in Rhineheld's and my other advisors' hands. Figuratively, at least.

Some things never change.

But in other respects? Wolf-god, *everything* has changed.

After my ever-increasing demands for Avila's hand, Rhineheld has stopped letting me run off at these meetings the way he did when I was younger. Now I have to sit through them all while gritting my teeth at how he makes choices for our estate and Lineage without my input, and often against my desires. Being forced to actually attend the meetings, not to mention suffering everyone's vigilance now that they are aware of my feelings for Avila, has made it harder to actually meet with him, but we still manage a few hours a day, usually after dinner and before the bedtime bells.

Though my council believes, and my father's will states, that I'm too young still to make choices for the continuation of my line, Rhineheld has decided I *am* old enough for *him* to make those decisions for me. While he can't make me marry, he can match me for breeding an unmarried omega in heat, and he's chosen one for next month—his own son, the pretty Miracules whom Avila once called arrogant. He's also begun putting together lists of prospective mid-Lineage omegas from other families for me to mate with and breed for additional political advantages.

I'm ashamed to admit I both want to do it, and I don't. Miracules *is* very handsome—strong, smart, well-formed, and he flirts with me constantly at home. I admit I'm also simply intrigued by lascivious thoughts of fucking and knotting and *pleasure*, and I do have fantasies of becoming a father...

But I want to share all that with Avila.

However, Rhineheld and my advisors block my way. They stand to make many more political connections by pimping out my seed for several years, than if I marry a Rossi omega of only average standing now and put an end to smaller alliances. They've even said they'd rather see me take one of Avila's younger omega brothers, someone my age, someone they say is *"riper,"* as my probable future omega. But I refuse.

It's Avila or no one.

JOURNAL! THE WORLD is amazing! Life is wonderful! The most extraordinary thing has happened!

You know I love and adore Avila, but I admit I've never known for sure how Avila feels about me! But this evening has changed everything! The world has tipped on its axis! The sun shines at night! Because a few hours ago, in the same spot where we first met by the river, Avila let me kiss him, and I swear, my soul left my body.

He let me kiss him and run my hands through his long black hair.

He let me touch his nipples beneath his white tunic.

He let me suck a wet kiss onto his neck.

He let me hold the length of his cock and slide my fingers around to his hole where he was wet with slick. For *me*.

I was out of my mind with need and want. My cock was so hard I nearly lost my load just touching him. Avila was hard, too, and he moved against my hand as if seeking release. Wolf-god, my fingers came close—*so close*—to sliding into him.

Oh, I'm hard again just writing about it.

If it hadn't been for the warning bell going off, announcing an omega was missing during bed check—Avila, obviously—we might have done more. I don't know why he allowed me to do even this much. I only asked to kiss him because if I am persuaded to mate and breed Miracules, I didn't want to knot another man without having at least kissed someone I care about first.

No, without having kissed *Avila* first.

I wanted to have that first pleasure with him and only him.

So I told him all that as we stood in the moonlight by the river, and he looked at me with wet eyes, before leaning toward me with a soft sob. He had to tilt his head down, because I'm still not as tall as him, and I took his motion for the offer it was—

His kiss was delicious. I want to feed on his lips for the rest of my life.

Oh, journal, I don't know what to do. I don't want to go through this heat with Miracules! I don't want to make children with anyone else at all! No matter how good it would be for my Lineage, for the diversity of our race, or for the political ties my advisors care so much for, I only want Avila.

And the way he clung to me as I kissed and touched him made me think he truly wants me, too. That he isn't just indulging the absurd crush of the little alpha who has chased him for years. But, like I said, before I could make him come, and before I could ask if he even wanted me to, the omega bed check bell rang, and he pulled away from me, eyes wide and full of fear. He ran away into the forest before I could get my erection under control enough to follow him. By the time I chased after him on the trail back to the main estate, he was long gone.

I hope he isn't in trouble for missing bed check.

I hope I see him over breakfast in the morning with the rest of the combined houses.

I hope he doesn't regret letting me kiss him and touch him.

More than anything else, I hope to kiss him again.

CHAPTER TWO

Year 654 of Wolf

VALE HAD STARTED reading the diary both out of necessity (requiring a primary source to back up his thesis paper) but also to impress Henry and find out more about the lonely librarian alpha. Now, though, he was so invested in Sian's story he couldn't stop thinking of it even as he helped Henry wrap the book up again and put it back into the box.

"You can come back tomorrow," Henry assured him, when Vale sighed. "It'll still be here."

"Will you be here too?" Vale asked.

Henry gave him a long look and then nodded. "I'm here most days."

"And when you're not? Where do you go?"

"I have a home," he said with a chuckle. "Mont Juror isn't the be-all and end-all of my existence."

"And do you have an omega?" Vale asked, his heart beating fast. "At your home?"

Henry studied him another long moment before

admitting, "I'm not the sort of alpha an omega would want."

Vale swallowed. He wanted to ask why, but maybe that was too personal. Maybe that would be hurtful to Henry. "But you believe in love?" He motioned at the box containing Sian's journal. "Don't you want it for yourself?"

"I definitely don't want what Sian and Avila had," Henry said with a laugh. "Their love was beautiful, but... Well, you'll see. It was brutal at times too. I like a quiet life."

"But—"

"Vale," Henry interrupted me. "Go on now. The journal will be here when you return."

Vale had no choice but to leave then, his mind whirling with questions about Henry, his home, and about Avila and Sian, and about love.

Vale had been taught his whole life that nothing was as powerful as a bond with an *Érosgápe*. No love as meaningful. It was the absolute pinnacle of human attachment, and it was the romantic dream of every omega to find their one-and-only beloved. A non-*Érosgápe*-based romance paled in comparison.

And yet...

Sian certainly seemed to adore his Avila with his whole heart.

The next day, as Henry unwrapped Sian and

Avila's book, he murmured, "You asked if I have an omega."

Vale's heart almost leapt out of his chest, but he tried to seem calm as he murmured, "Oh? Do you?"

"I told you yesterday I'm not the sort of alpha an omega wants."

"I think you could be," Vale said, heat in his cheeks. "If he were the right omega. Someone understanding. Someone with poetry in them?" He thought he might combust from sheer embarrassment and his rapid-fire pulse.

Henry set the journal down between them, watching as Vale touched the cover with shaking hands. Oh, wolf-god, how they betrayed him! And his hot face, too!

"Do you think you're the right omega?"

Vale felt himself go hot all over as if his body had erupted into flames. The chair, wolf-god damn it, didn't sink into the floor and take him with it.

"That's unfair of me," Henry said with a small smile. "Look, you're a beautiful young man."

Vale knew he was, his dark hair against his fair skin was a nice contrast, and then he had true, moss-green eyes, which his father called a miracle. He was a good-looking omega. Any alpha would be happy to have him. Or so his pater insisted.

Henry went on. "But I do have someone."

"You do?"

Henry nodded. "His name is Caden, and I love him very much. While we don't share the kind of love that burns as hot as Sian's passion for Avila, we are happy." He laughed a little. "We're comfortable in our love. He's a beta."

"A beta," Vale murmured.

"Our relationship is…"

"Not forbidden," Vale said quietly. Unlike alpha with alpha, or omega with omega, an alpha with a beta was considered odd but it was not utterly verboten.

"Caden doesn't have needs I can't ever meet."

Vale stared at Henry's beautiful gray eyes. So the rumors were true. Henry couldn't knot an omega. Vale's heart cracked a little. Henry could never knot *him*, even if he were to somehow lure him away from this Caden. Even if Henry thought Vale was beautiful and desired him. Even if they weren't years and years apart, and at different places in life.

Not that Henry gave any impression of feeling anything like that.

But still…

The revelation was crushing.

Vale wished Henry had never said a word. He preferred his dreams and fantasies. They were safe enough, harmless. Why had he told him?

"We have a house by the river," Henry went on, eyes distant as if picturing the house in his mind. His smile was fond. "Caden likes to fish. He has that in common with Sian. And I like to paint. We're quiet people. Love doesn't have to be so all-or-nothing—like with *Érosgápe*, or like with Sian and Avila. It can come in all shapes and sizes."

"Then why do you like their story so much?" Vale asked. He sounded a little angry and he was pretty sure the room was blurry because of the stubborn tears in his eyes.

"Because life is hard, and they survived it. This journal gave me courage when I needed it. I hope you can gain strength from it too."

"I'm here to get information for my term paper," Vale reminded him, though they both knew that wasn't the whole story.

"Yes. And for the edification of your heart."

Then he left him to it.

Vale opened the journal to where he'd left off, dizzy with misery. He'd been such a fool.

A fool with a stupid crush.

Now, with just a few words from Henry, it was all ruined.

45

Sian Maxima's Journal
Year 136 of Wolf

EVERYTHING IS RUINED. My life is over. I want to die, but I can't, because I have to find a way to fix things for Avila.

That's all that matters now.

He's all that matters.

JOURNAL, I'M SORRY to have been so dramatic in my last entry, though the drama was warranted in every way. Everything is ruined, and I do have to find a way to fix things for Avila.

See, the thing is, according to his father, I've ruined him with my dick, which I hadn't even known was possible, and yet—

Let me start at the beginning. If I can. I don't know. I just want to scream and rant and rip my hair out, but Avila's brother, Scorpius, tells me that's the very last thing I should be doing right now.

So I will refrain. Barely.

Last night, I knotted Avila. Oh, wait, that's the end. Let me go back to the beginning.

I met him by the river last night, as we usually do during the month of meetings. I was already excited to see him, full of memories of our kiss, and wondering if he'd be willing to kiss me again. But when Avila arrived, he was different somehow, flushed and smelling like the best thing in the world. I was immediately aroused, and I told him so. The words just burst out of me before I could stop them.

"I'm going into heat soon," Avila replied. His long hair lifted with the night breeze, and he smelled so, so, *so* divine.

I don't think he meant to be coy with me, but his dark lashes fluttered as he said it, and he bit into his lower lip. That ignited me even more. "I'll have to be in the heat house starting tomorrow. I wanted to say goodbye to you, Sian. I won't see you again until next year."

"'Heat,'" I repeated dumbly, because, honestly, I felt quite dumb in the presence of his glowing, fair-skinned, black-haired beauty, especially with all that scent of slick swirling around me. I was lightheaded and hard, and I hadn't even touched him.

"Yes. I think that's why I let you last night."

"Why you 'let' me…?" I admit that somehow the night before had gone flat out of my mind in the face of all his present deliciousness. I couldn't even summon the memory of touching him for all the need to touch him at that moment.

"Not that I don't care about you, Sian. I do. I'd have let you kiss me even without the oncoming heat if you'd ever tried before last night. But I do think it made it absolutely impossible to tell you no."

"Impossible to say no?"

"Stop repeating what I'm saying."

"You smell like heaven."

"Thank you." Avila blushed. "I wanted to see you again, to ask you, to *beg* you... Please don't mate another omega, especially not Miracules. *Please.* I know it's not fair to ask you to make this promise, but..." He took a shuddering breath. "I hate the thought of you knotted in another man."

"I hate it, too."

"I need to go now," Avila said breathlessly when I stepped closer, my hands already reaching for him. "I just wanted to say goodbye and make that unfair request."

"Why is it unfair?" I asked, slipping my fingers into his glossy hair. He moaned as I slid them down the length of it and tugged at the ends. It was so soft.

"Because I'd take another alpha's knot for this heat if they'd let me," he whispered. "Not because I want another alpha, but because..." He closed his eyes as I stroked his neck and up to his smooth cheeks. Omegas don't always have smooth cheeks, but he does. I love how soft they are. "Because it hurts so much without a knot," he whispered, his throat clicking around a desperate swallow. "I'm sorry, Sian. I wish I could say otherwise. It's wrong to beg you not to breed with another omega when I'd allow—"

"Shh," I commanded, putting my fingers on his lips. They were soft. "I will never let another alpha knot you."

He nodded, eyes wet as he looked down. "Father says he's saving me in case you *do* still want me when you're of age. So you don't have to worry. My body is for you only."

I don't know why, journal, but when he said that—*"my body is for you only"*—I lost my mind. I kissed him. He kissed me back. I grabbed him close, and we moved together, desperately, both of us hard and straining instantly, and when I started to tug his white tunic up, he pulled away. "I'm sorry, I know you said you'd never..." Avila murmured. "But it's the only private place."

I knew exactly where he meant.

I followed him up the hill to the heat houses and into the one he'd shown me before. The door was scored with more nail marks, and the room was barren of even a bed.

His skin was hot. My hands were all over him. I don't remember taking his clothes off, but I remember the glow of his white skin in the warm evening's moonlight and the way his moans rose and fell as I kissed him everywhere, making love-vows, and demanding for our bodies to meld into one so we could never be separated.

Perhaps all that demanding was what ruined me.

Wolf-god has no love for hubris.

I can't express the joy that consumed me when he pulled me down to that packed earth and spread his legs for me. The heat and tightness of him was unreal. I gasped as I pushed inside, and he clung to me like a wild thing as I moved in him.

I will always remember his every gasp. Every sigh. I wrung so many lovely noises out of him as we kissed and pulsed together like *Érosgápe* do. I felt a union with him like none I'd ever imagined. We are *not Érosgápe*, I know, and yet when I came inside him, a full-throated cry issuing from my very core, and I felt him come too, I believed he and I were absolutely of one soul. Avila convulsed around my cock, and spurted between our bodies, and clawed at my back like a beautiful, sweet, perfect omega in heat.

And he *was* in heat, journal.

He was.

In my lust for him, I'd lost control, and I only came to my senses as I lay panting on top of him, knotted hard inside him, and trembling all over.

He came to his senses, too, but only for a few moments…

"Oh, little alpha, I didn't mean for you to knot me," he whispered, kissing my mouth gently. And then his eyes rolled back, his body trembled under me, and he was lost to his pleasure again.

My knot didn't deflate for a very long time, and Avila twisted on it, coming again and again. I watched him avidly. My beautiful Avila, my stunning heart, my everything.

And that's when it all went wrong.

Voices. A hunt for us both had begun. I was knotted inside him still. He was still lost to his heat.

My heart pounded. My blood ran cold.

Perhaps it was fear that finally made my knot go down, but it was too late.

The door burst open, and we were surrounded.

Avila was still gone, deep in his heat, but they dragged me off him, and one of the men who'd found us kicked him in the stomach. I screamed, lunging, but it was useless. I'm still a small alpha. The men holding me were some of Rossi's oldest alpha sons, including the brute Valter. They spat on their omega brother, called him horrible names, and lifted him—senseless though he was—to punch him. I struggled, screaming at them to leave him alone, to stop hurting him, and then I begged for them to let me service him.

His brothers turned on me then, dragging me away from the hut. I pleaded to be allowed to help Avila, to care for him through the heat, until Valter punched me so hard I was knocked out. I remember nothing else until I was halfway down the hill, being pulled from beneath my arms, between two more of Avila's alpha brothers, my legs dragging.

It only grew worse from there.

My own council called me things so foul I'd never heard them spoken aloud in my life. But worse was the Rossi family's take on what had occurred: they said I had dishonored Avila. That I'd ruined him. That he was worthless now and would be banished to the heat house forever.

Forever.

I can't fathom it.

Dama, my friend, and the only one of the advisors of my Lineage whom I've always thought had some sense in his head, told me the best thing we could do for Avila right now was to leave the estate immediately, even before the month-long meeting was over.

"I have to help him," I yelled, pacing restlessly as Dama packed our things. The beta servants I'd been granted by the Rossi household moved back and forth between rooms, organizing the decampment of my entire group of people. "I love him."

"If you love him, you'll leave."

"What if I don't leave? What if I go to his father and say, Leader Rossi, I love your son, and—"

"You've said that for years. He knows it already. He held the boy aside for you." Dama threw his hands in the air. "And you were too impatient! You couldn't wait! You put your alpha cock in his sweet hole out of sheer lust and that's it. It doesn't take more than that for them. Don't you get it? The Rossi aren't just old-fashioned, they're puritanical, and they will *not* let this pass for either of you."

"What's so wrong with what we did?"

"Nothing!" he said, tossing my favorite book of poetry on top of all the others in my trunk and shutting it. "If you'd chosen an omega of any other Lineage—Sabel, Chase, Monhundy, Laken, whoever—there would have been nothing wrong with what you did, aside from the fact you didn't make proper arrangements for it. Most Lineage Leaders would have even seen it as an obligation— an alpha servicing an omega through an unexpected heat. But the Rossi are puritanical to a fault, Sian, which I've told you, and others have told you for years. They see an omega as spoiled forever once touched."

I argued with him, like it made any difference. Like he could change anything at all. "But it's our obligation to procreate, to make children for wolf-god, and I want to make them with Avila—"

"We know."

That was when it hit me, a sensation both hot and cold moving through my body. "And I might! We did! He could have my child in him!"

"If he does, they'll allow him to deliver it, and send it to us."

I swallowed feeling dizzy and hopeful. "Then he can come to me?"

Dama shook his head. "That's not how the Rossi work."

I stamped my foot like a child. "When can he come to me?"

Dama shouted. "Do you want to start a war?"

"We can't go to war," I said. "We are too few. Wolf-god abhors war. We need every last person."

"We do, and yet Gregorus Rossi has a different view of wolf-god, and he believes purity is what wolf-god loves best." Dama took a slow breath, running his hands through his pale hair. "Plus, you betrayed his trust, his faith in you and our Lineage. As far as he's concerned, you took his son without sanction. He's lost a valuable asset—"

"Avila is a man, not an asset!"

"To Gregorus Rossi, good omegas are one of three things: assets, virgins, or paters. Anything else is a whore."

"A *what*?"

"An omega who is used for pleasure in exchange for money."

"I know what a whore is! I'm saying how is Avila, who only gave in because I asked, who only let me have him because he was in heat, who was only with me because he just wanted to tell me goodbye—how is he a whore?"

"You and I know he's not. But the Rossi feel differently because they believe in wolf-god's directive toward purity over all else."

I ground my teeth in rage. "Wolf-god only told us to be pure unto each other. That's not the same thing as 'omegas must remain virgins until marriage no matter how painful or awful it is.'"

"The Rossi believe many twisted things."

"Like?"

"Like, while wolf-god was kind to give us omegas to save humanity after the loss of the Old World's women, omegas go through heat and die in childbirth as a punishment."

"Why would they need to be punished? For being an omega? We need them!"

"Because the Rossi believe they are the returned

souls of the damned women from the before-times."

"What kind of sick—"

Dama slammed his fist against the chest he'd just packed for me. "You'd know all this if you'd listened in the meetings instead of daydreaming about your pretty omega."

"I *did* listen, when it pertained to us, to our Lineage!"

"That's not what being a leader is, Sian," he shouted at me. "You have to listen to everything, to know the best way to act for all, so we can move forward together as a society. The Rossi have made it clear for years they have no intention of changing their draconian ways. There's only so much we can do. Like you said, war isn't an option."

But I felt like starting a war, journal.

I felt like setting fire to the entire Rossi estate. I was shaking and livid and ready to do just that. But Dama talked me down.

"You can't help him if you stay or do something crazy," Dama said gently. "Your only chance is to leave now, make a plan, and act on it. There will be a way to save him, to take him for your own. I believe that. But it's impossible right now. If you love him, you can't leave it to chance. You must make a good plan. In the meantime…"

I knew he was right. "I have to go."

"Yes."

So we went.

I thought I could hear wails coming from the hills, as we took the long drive past the Rossi gates and out to the road that would eventually lead to the Maxima estate. I felt sure I could hear my beloved's agony as he sweated through his heat without a knot, without an alpha who could take care of him. But when I asked Dama if he heard anything, he simply said, "It's in your head, Sian. It's all in your head. Let's get you home. You can let your own screams out there."

And I did, journal. I most certainly did.

CHAPTER THREE

Year 654 of Wolf

VALE SAT BENEATH the oak tree in the main courtyard, watching as his friends pushed, shoved, and begged their way to the counters of the new food stands the administration had allowed to be erected for the week before the summer solstice.

There was a stand for sausages, another selling grilled cheese sandwiches, and a third with desserts galore. The weather was warm, and the breeze rushed down through the green, forested hills to offset the heat. All of the omegas at Mont Juror were wearing their lightest shirts and pants. A few daring seniors were even wearing shorts, which hadn't been banned outright by the school's dress code, but were still discouraged as too provocative to be decent.

But they were all omegas here—with a few betas, like those running the food stands and acting as staff on campus. No alphas were on campus to become aroused by the sight of exposed, hairy omega legs. Unless he counted Henry—no, *Mr.*

Marks. He was an alpha, but one deemed safe by the school due to his "accident."

Vale sipped his lemonade and bit into the grilled cheese sandwich he'd bought earlier and thought about Mr. Marks. He was still embarrassed to have been so easily read and called out on his crush, but he supposed it was for the best. There was no future for them, not only because Hen—no, *Mr. Marks*—was much older, but because Vale still held out hope for an *Érosgápe* mate. If he couldn't have that, he hoped to one day find an alpha who would love him the way Sian loved Avila.

Mr. Marks didn't seem to want a love like that—a swoony, desperate, all-consuming love. He was satisfied with something softer, something easier. Vale didn't think he could ever settle for a love so tepid. Though he hoped to wolf-god he didn't have to endure the same amount of pain Avila did before his alpha could take him home.

After the humiliation with Mr. Marks, he'd decided he would skim the journal for the information he needed for his paper and get out of the library for good. But before long he'd again found himself absorbed in Sian and Avila's problems. He'd read the entirety of the journal over the prior week, too immersed in their trials and tribulations to let his own shame at having a crush on Mr. Marks prevent him from going back to the library every chance he got.

Vale hadn't been able to get many of the diary's passages out of his mind.

It wasn't just the lasciviousness of some of Sian's thoughts and memories that intrigued him—though there were some generous sensual descriptions, of course. Vale may have even taken himself in hand when he was alone in the shower, touched his soft anus, and imagined himself in Avila's position, beneath an ardent alpha (not Mr. Marks!) gasping with desire. But there were so many other parts of Sian and Avila's story he didn't want to imagine for himself. Pain, suffering, and fear. He understood what Mr. Marks had meant about all that now. And yet he hadn't been able to stop himself from poring over the pages, feeling everything Sian and Avila felt. He envied their love, and wished he could turn back time and change things for them.

If only they had been born today...

It was true times had changed, but they hadn't changed nearly enough. Vale was still required to *"keep himself to himself,"* as his instructors put it, code for staying a virgin, until a solid attempt had been made at finding his *Érosgápe* or securing a good contract with another alpha. That wouldn't happen for a few more years.

In the meantime, they doled out heat suppressants to keep him from enduring the rigors of heat without an alpha. Once it was determined an omega's *Érosgápe* would likely never be found, and a suitable contract could not be made, it was typically every omega for himself. Heat suppressants were ripped away. Institutional support was utterly removed. They were left abandoned.

At that point, omegas were required to find an alpha friend to handle their heats with no strings attached, or they were obliged to spend an exorbitant amount of money on hired alphas to service their needs—typically those alphas who'd made a profession out of it. Which meant omegas often ended up enduring heats with paid strangers. And, of course, sometimes heats came with no plan in place at all. Accidental breedings happened, and babies were born with their father unknown. Sometimes, even worse things occurred.

Still, it *was* better today than in Sian and Avila's time. Vale shuddered, thinking of the agony omegas like Avila had gone through in the early days of wolf without the aid of heat suppressants, forced to sweat out their youthful heats with no help. Others had been brutalized by groups of alphas competing for access to their heats while the omegas were too out of it to defend themselves. The Lineages of yore could be puritanical, it was true, but they typically protected their omegas from rape at least.

Finishing his sandwich, Vale decided to return to the library. He wanted to read the journal again. There was something so compelling in Sian's handwritten pages. If that kind of love did exist, it was worth enduring anything life threw at him to find it. At least Mr. Marks wasn't working today, so he could spare himself the torment of his own blushes.

Once the old leather journal was in front of him, and Vale was alone with Sian and Avila again, he took a deep, reverent breath before opening it. He made sure none of the pouches that someone—had it been Sian himself?—had carefully sewn into some of the inside pages fell open and none of their precious contents—old letters, a few locks of hair— fell out.

Scanning the first entries after Sian had confessed his love for Avila, he decided to skip to the middle of their story. On his first read-through, he'd agonized every step of the way with Sian and Avila, but with the sun shining through the big window, he found he didn't want to relive Sian's agony as he waited a full month for news of Avila, denied at every turn by the Rossi family.

Instead, Vale cut straight to the entries where

Avila's fate was at last revealed.

Sian Maxima's Journal
Year 137 of Wolf

AT SOME POINT over the next few weeks, I am supposed to breed Miracules. As soon as his heat comes, which could be any day, Rhineheld is adamant that I service his son. Apparently, it's always been his plan ever since we were youngsters for us to share our first heat experiences together. I've already shared my first experience with Avila, but Rhineheld is resolute that Miracules will take my knot. Dama is trying to talk me into it. He says the pleasure will be good for me, and I'll make a better, more experienced alpha for Avila when we are able to free him. But I think that's a lie. I think he's just trying to distract me.

I suggested as much, and he said, "It would go a long way to prove your devotion to Avila isn't solely about an immature attachment to the first omega who let you knot them. Believe me, there are plenty on our estate and amongst the advisors who believe that's what's going on here. They think if you mate with another, you'll move on."

But I won't do it. They can't make me. Mate *or*

move on.

They'll soon see I'm serious about Avila and no one else.

There is a knock at my door…

JOURNAL, I HAVE much to tell you. I finally have news of Avila.

The knock at my door was a servant alerting me to the arrival of Scorpius, one of Avila's brothers. He is the second oldest alpha of the Rossi Lineage and has many opinions about the way the estate and the Lineage are being handled by his father and elder brother these days.

But I get ahead of myself.

The good news is Avila is all right. He is alive and has recovered from his heat and his brothers' initial injuries to his body.

However, the bad news is he is still confined to the heat house. It's been over a month now. I feel ill at the thought of him locked in that darkness. No, not ill, enraged. If it were not for Scorpius's wise counsel, I might have left mid-meeting and taken a horse directly to the Rossi estate and attempted to break in to spirit him away.

But, again, I'm ahead of myself.

There is even more news.

Avila is pregnant.

I don't know how to feel about that. I am the father, obviously, and I want the child and Avila both, but I am full of absolute horror at how they are keeping Avila in the meantime, and I'm full of fear over what Scorpius tells me the plan will be to change his circumstances.

But let me start at the beginning.

I left my writing here and went down to the receiving room, shaking from head to toe with hope and anger and fear when the beta servant informed me Scorpius was here. He'd come alone and asked that I meet with him alone as well. It was night, and the rest of the household had gone to bed, so his request was easily accommodated.

When I walked into the room, the servants had lit a fire, and he stood in front of it, facing the door, hands clasped behind his back and looking every bit the master of the room. I felt small—how I wish I would grow!—and young as I approached him, but I tried to put on a brave front.

"Have you brought him to me?" I demanded. Since I'd sent daily letters demanding Avila be sent to me, I had allowed myself a breath of hope that Avila's father had given in, and Scorpius was here to deliver him.

Instead, he laughed, and said, "You arrogant little shit. Sit the fuck down, shut up, and listen."

Journal, I wish I could say I protested his treatment of me in my own home, but I was so desperate to hear of Avila that I obeyed.

"Good," he said, nodding and sipping the drink someone had supplied him with, no doubt a beta servant. "Now, if you want my little brother—"

"I do!"

"Then you'll have to be far smarter than you have been so far."

That was what Dama told me all the time, too. "But how?"

I am only nineteen, and I haven't paid nearly enough attention at the meetings I've been forced to attend, and I've let Rhineheld handle the harder parts of leadership here at home. I now regret every hour I've spent in fun over the last few years.

"My brother is pregnant with your possible heir," he pointed out.

"He..." I felt dizzy and was glad I was sitting down. The news was overwhelming. "He is?"

"Yes. If you had to do something so stupid, this is the best possible outcome for Avila."

"It is?" I was dazed. My beloved is pregnant with my child. But he is locked away where I can't protect him, hold him, keep him nourished and safe through the pregnancy, satisfy his every whim and need.

"Pay attention!" Scorpius snapped, crossing his strong arms over his chest, flexing his muscles. "For wolf-god's sake, did Avila have to choose such a child?" he muttered under his breath. "Listen to me. You cannot let them take the upper hand. You can't allow your advisors to simply agree that my father may send the baby to you when it's born."

"What other choice do I have?"

"Many. You must make an enormous stink about this. You must rage and storm that your heir is at risk. You must insist first on better accommodations for Avila during his pregnancy, and then for your son to remain with him until he can be naturally weaned according to wolf-god's laws—and you must assert that he cannot be fully weaned for three years."

I immediately saw the wisdom in insisting Avila be given better accommodations. I knew instantly that if my demands—as outlined by Scorpius—were met then Avila's situation would be much improved until I can get him out of there. But surely it will not take three years to free him? Still, for the first time, thanks to Scorpius, I can see a glimmer of light. Not only do I have a way to improve Avila's current conditions, but I know I have a partner in Scorpius.

I spent half the night with him, listening to his plans, agreeing to do as he commanded. In the wee hours, I offered him a room for rest, but he declined, saying it would look too friendly if he were seen staying at my estate. Our alliance must be secret for now.

He has his own motivations, aside from brotherly love—which I'm glad to report he does have for Avila. He is cultivating political power, something I haven't cared about enough myself, until now. But as Scorpius rightfully pointed out, that must change if I wish to save Avila from more pain.

Before he left, I asked him to carry a letter to Avila for me. He agreed, and though I didn't have much time, I quickly jotted down my feelings and devotion. I didn't mention the plan. It's too risky since he would have no way to destroy the letter— unless he ate it? I don't want him to eat it. The ink might not be good for him or the baby.

Whatever the case, I told Scorpius to tell Avila we are going to save him.

He clapped me on the shoulder and said, "I see you do love him. But love is pointless, you idiot. Now you need to earn him."

I suppose he's right. And I will. I will do everything I can to earn Avila's safety and comfort.

At any cost.

CHAPTER FOUR

Year 656 of Wolf

VALE STOOD OUTSIDE the darkened library, staring at the doors, wishing he had a way to enter. It'd been nearly a year and a half since he'd last read Sian's journal, but he really wanted—no, *needed*—to read it again. He needed to know, despite everything, despite disappointments, that life did go on, and joy could be found.

Love was out there.

The last dance of the Class of Wolf-storm's Debut Tour had ended an hour before, and, yet again Vale had found himself unclaimed. At first, as his class had started their travels, going from city-to-city and town-to-town, dancing with alphas, meeting as many unbonded men as possible, it had all seemed like a grand adventure. He'd seen so many new faces, and been introduced to new customs and lands.

But in the end, it was all pointless because he was alone.

Jordy had found his *Érosgápe* in Calter, of all places. Not even at a Wolf-storm Debut Dance, but at a stop along the roadside, licking an ice cream and not expecting his alpha to appear as if out of thin air next to him. It'd been intense. Almost violent. They'd nearly coupled there on the ground, and had it not been for the other alphas around, and the leaders of the Wolf-storm Debut Progression, they'd have consummated their bond immediately.

Vale hadn't seen Jordy again after that, though he'd had a letter from him reporting all was well, that he was happy and looking forward to his first heat with his beloved.

Even Yonder had been claimed. It was the fourth Wolf-storm Debut Dance, somewhere near the mountains, and a rough fellow had come in with his coarse alpha-pals, and *boom*. Instant. At least when alphas came to a Debut Dance everyone was ready for a potential *Érosgápe* pairing, so the two were separated, the alpha dosed with alpha quell, and their parents summoned to arrange the contract.

All in all, the average had held true. Around thirty-five percent of Vale's class had found an *Érosgápe* mate, and the rest of them…had not.

Vale stood outside the library in the darkness, listening to the sounds of his unclaimed friends all around the courtyard, reuniting with family, making plans to attend Philia Committee soirées in hopes of locating a compatible alpha to contract with, and generally feeling much better than he did about their futures.

His own parents would never arrive. He'd received the horrible news two months before his graduation. His father and pater had died in a freak accident. A runaway fire truck had struck them both and they'd died at the scene. He'd sobbed himself to sleep for a month, and then he'd gone to the library, read Sian and Avila's story again, and decided it was time to carry on.

From that point on, he'd lived for the Wolfstorm Debut Progression and the hope of finding his *Érosgápe*. Now, with the disappointment of failure as heavy as a stone in his chest, the pain of his loss welled up again. It was clear what was going to happen to him now. He'd return to his family's home alone, live there alone, and even die there alone.

The pain was gutting. Why he couldn't cry, he didn't know, but no tears came, only a dry, hollow despair.

Tonight, he'd sleep alone in his old dorm room, and then say goodbye to Mont Juror forever. Without parents to argue and petition on his behalf, they'd remove his access to heat suppressants.

Within a month he'd experience his first heat. He'd need to find an alpha to help him through it. He didn't know many, and none he'd be willing to ask to provide so intimate a service.

Vale was terrified of losing control of himself in front of someone who knew him, much less someone he didn't know at all. An omega in heat… So many bad things could go wrong if the wrong alpha was there for it. Not the least of which was an unwanted pregnancy from an alpha who'd agreed to use a condom and then did not.

Of course, there were Mont Juror services for matching omegas to alphas for heats. Those services, unlike the suppressants, would continue for as long as he required them. But it was all so scary and strange.

Fill out a form, hire an alpha, be stripped down to his very soul in front of him? Over and over? Lost to boundaries or consent? Terrifying.

If his parents had lived, that would've been their job—to help him find a suitable alpha for his heats. They'd have made sure he liked the man, was friendly with him beforehand, and…

What good was wishing now?

It was like standing on the steps and wishing for a way into the library. Hopeless.

It didn't matter how desperately he wanted to be

sitting at the wooden desks in the Reserved Room, safely wrapped up in history's problems, re-reading the pages of Sian's journal and Avila's accompanying letters...

To fantasize and dream. To lose himself in *their* agony and pain instead of his own.

To read of an omega who withstood so much suffering and still found a way to embrace a love that wasn't *"destined"* or *"fated"* but was beautiful all the same. To find inspiration in their story and a path toward hope.

He couldn't now.

He should return to his dorm room and face reality. It wasn't too late to start planning how to deal with his problems. As horrible as it sounded, he should submit his information to the matching service, or suck it up and begin to ask his friends if they had any kind and willing alpha brothers or cousins who might help him at a reasonable rate.

Vale needed to stop pretending. There was no alpha savior out there for him, no *Érosgápe* mate to sweep him off his feet and into eternal bliss. It was just him, facing an uncertain future on the verge of his first heat. He had no choice but to raise his chin, make hard choices, and march on.

Alone.

Sian Maxima's Journal
Year 137 of Wolf

JOURNAL, I HAVE a real problem.

Wait, wait, excuse me while I laugh myself sick because my entire life is a real problem at this point. I guess the better way to put it is I have a *new* real problem.

Except Miracules isn't new.

I've known for a long time Rhineheld has plans to use my seed as his way to hold on to power even after I've passed into the age of majority. He knows he can do so if he can convince me to handle Miracules's upcoming heat and *if* Miracules becomes pregnant with my child. It's clear to me that Rhineheld has long cherished hopes for me to fall for Miracules's charms—and Miracules has many; he's quite handsome with very nice eyes— and offer to wed him. Most of all, he wishes for a grandson of his to become my heir. I would be bound to Rhineheld by a stronger tie than loyalty.

Or so he assumes.

I'm ashamed to say it took Scorpius spelling all this out for me to see the full truth. I'd always known Rhineheld wanted me to handle Miracules's heat for political reasons, yes. I'm not that stupid.

But I hadn't realized how far his ambitions reached, or that he hoped strongly for a pregnancy right away, and not just a pleasantly passed heat for his son and a good learning experience for me. I now see, of course, that this has long played into Rhineheld's position that I am too young to marry Avila.

I should have realized.

Scorpius also told me Rhineheld will not support me in my agitations for better conditions for Avila because he hopes that Avila will lose our child, and Miracules will have a chance to become pregnant with my first child instead. Should that child be an alpha—which, unlike omegas, can't be known until the signs present themselves—and *if* my future omega by marriage delivers no alphas for me, then Rhineheld's grandchild would still be my heir.

So this is the hardest part of the plan Scorpius and I have concocted—no, not the hardest, for that role goes to Avila, without his consent and against his will, I'm afraid—but it is a difficult part of our plan for me to swallow: I must use Rhineheld's ambitions against him.

He can't force me to fuck his son through his upcoming heat—though, should he force me into a room with Miracules and lock me in, it would be incredibly hard to resist the scent and need of him. Which is where Scorpius comes in. He's gotten his hands on a new medicine, something called alpha quell, which keeps an alpha's urges in check, allowing them to stay rational during a heat. Apparently, it also helps when two *Érosgápe* find each other, restraining the urges from the *Érosgápe* connection so nothing imprudent is done before a marriage is undertaken.

But I've swerved away from the topic yet again.

I must tell Rhineheld I will not handle his son's heat unless he helps me achieve better accommodations for Avila. If he agrees and manages the negotiation, then I'll handle Miracules's heat, even though I don't wish to. It's a fair trade.

If Rhineheld refuses? Then I am to refuse as well, even to the point of being with Miracules in a heat house and listening to his screams. Even to the point of refusing to relieve his agony. The alpha quell will help me manage it physically, but emotionally I must hold strong. It will be hard. I feel ill imagining it, and yet I must remember that, thanks in part to Rhineheld's stubbornness and ambition, my Avila has sweated through multiple heats unassisted, and even now is locked in a dark Rossi heat house while pregnant with my son.

So, though Miracules is not to blame, and I wish

no harm on him, as he's quite beautiful and has always been kind to me, if Rhineheld stays stubborn, so will I.

I will let Miracules suffer if I must.

For Avila.

JOURNAL, THE DEED is done.

It only took one day of his son's screams for Rhineheld to relent. It took an additional day and a half on his fastest horse for him to reach the Rossi estate, and another day for a messenger to return with a promise from Gregorus Rossi that Avila would be moved at once to a heat house for married omegas, though he will still be denied visitors of any kind. The letter was closed with the Rossi seal.

I mounted Miracules within minutes of reading the letter. His screams were more than I could bear, and I still wake in the night shaking with the horror of what I did to him. I pray he will forgive me, but I understand if he cannot. Eventually, I did my duty by him, and I pray to wolf-god he is not pregnant. I confess the process was enjoyable. The sensations were undeniable. But I resent I was used in such a way, and I loathe seeing Miracules waltzing about our estate now that it is over, looking pleased and radiant, knowing that Avila—whom I would much rather have spent several days pleasuring—is suffering still.

At least I know he is in a real house now.

I await news from Scorpius so we can execute the next step of our plan.

But I swear to wolf-god above, I will never be used as a stud again. There is no pleasure worth the degradation of mating against my will.

The only omega I will touch in the future is Avila, Rhineheld's schemes be damned.

CHAPTER FIVE

Year 659 of Wolf

THREE YEARS AFTER leaving Mont Juror and failing to find his *Érosgápe* during the Wolf-storm Debut Tour, Vale strolled with his beta friend Rosen along a wide boardwalk by the sea. The water was topaz-blue, and the sky was full of fluffy white clouds that seemed to rush over their background of sun-pale blue.

"Ah, let's step in here," Vale said, indicating a bookstore with bright red and blue flags out front, waving in the sea breeze.

"Always a sucker for books," Rosen said fondly, following Vale inside and heading directly to the Art section as usual. Being a painter, he enjoyed reading about artists from the Old World as well as the new artists in wolf-god's world.

Vale preferred to peruse the stacks more haphazardly. His interests were far and wide, and he loved to read about almost any topic. First, he checked the shelves for books of his own poetry and was pleased to find a couple in stock: his first collection and his last. He wandered over to the history section, and then to the biographies. On a table between shelves there stood a stack of green books with gold letters embossed on the front.

The title caught his eye and Vale paused, his heart tripping over itself. It couldn't be…

It'd been years since he'd last read Sian's story.

Lifting the book, Vale found a familiar name on the cover. *Diary prepared for print by Henry Marks.* The first entry began just as Vale remembered, and he moved his lips as he read the words silently. It wasn't quite the same as holding the leather-bound journal itself, with its brittle, dry pages and reading Sian's strong handwriting, but it was amazing to have the story in his hands again.

Flipping through, he wondered how Avila's letters had been handled—or if they'd been included at all. Pleased, he found an appendix at the end with the contents of all the letters that had been sewn into the original. He skimmed them and found none were missing.

"Found something good?" Rosen asked at his elbow, reaching to pick up another copy.

"Yes. I read this journal in school. It's fascinating, really. A beautiful love story."

"Hmm," Rosen flipped through the book briefly, before setting it back on the stack. "I'm ready when you are. They don't have any Old World art books here that Yosef hasn't already bought for me."

"Spoiled," Vale murmured.

"Lucky."

With an agreeable nod, Vale chose another copy of the journal from the bottom of the stack, replacing the one he'd taken off the top. "I'm ready. Let's go."

Later that night, when Rosen and his beta lover Yosef had gone to bed, Vale moved out to the front porch of their rented house by the sea, with a flashlight so he could read alone in the darkness. He took deep breaths, enjoying the solitude, his only company the sound of the waves crashing onto the beach.

First, Vale read the beginning, savoring each word, reacquainting himself with Sian's arrogant childishness. But then he skipped ahead to the appendices, eager to re-read one of his favorite letters that had been sewn into the diary, one from Avila to Sian. Because the letters had come so rarely, Vale knew how Sian had cherished every one of them. He also loved the glimpses of Avila's point of view regarding his and Sian's story. Though the letters weren't always uplifting.

The difficulties Avila had faced were harrowing,

sad, and titillating to him, all at the same time. Sometimes he wondered if he was a bad person, in that he received such relief in reading about the miserable moments in Avila and Sian's lives, but the darkness of their history made everything he now faced seem so much easier to bear.

If that made him a bad person, then so be it. It hurt no one.

And in his own life he'd found that "hurting no one" was harder than he'd ever imagined it to be.

A Letter Sewn into Sian Maxima's Journal
Year 137 of Wolf

Dear Sian,

Scorpius has allowed me pen and paper and given a vow to deliver my words to you unread and unaltered.

He tells me that you know of the child. He grows well. The food they provide me is sufficient, and I am not ill any longer. Don't worry for my health.

I don't hold you responsible for what happened that day. I was aware my heat was coming upon me, and I should have gone to the heat house several days before. But I couldn't deny myself the pleasure of seeing you, knowing it would be another year before I would again. It was irresponsible of me. I apologize for putting you in such an impossible position.

I also don't hold you accountable for me. There were many youthful promises made over the years, but I was always the older of the two of us, and I always knew you would one day grow up and be forced to turn away from childish passions. That I, myself, was a childish passion.

I won't be crushed if you move on. I know even now you may be in the arms of another omega, someone more correct for you, someone your advisors approve of, and I want you to be happy if that's the case.

Scorpius tells me you are still true to me. But you don't need to be, Sian. You don't need to be.

You deserve a life with an omega who...

Well, with an omega who can actually be there with you, and wolf-god knows my father is never setting me free. I'm grateful for whatever you did to secure this new house for me. It's solid, safe, and while they removed the softest pillows and the mattress,

I am much more comfortable, I promise you.

So don't do anything you'll regret. When the child is born, I promise to love him and give him the best of me until it is time to send him to you.

Don't worry about me, Sian. I am well. I'll find a way to be content enough.

I want you to live a good life, a happy life.

Avila

JOURNAL, I RECEIVED a letter from Avila today and it broke my heart. He's obviously trying very hard to be brave—because he is a brave man—and doesn't want me to suspect how hard he is struggling. His brother, Scorpius, has made it clear, though: Avila is deeply unhappy, lonely, and frightened. Just hearing him confirm my suspicions made me tremble with rage.

I will repay these bastards for what they've done to him one day. And Rhineheld, too. But for now, I must be patient, while Scorpius works out the plot on his end of things. In a month's time, we can make our next move, when Avila's and my baby is born. Hard to believe I will be a father in only one more month. Hard to believe my beloved Avila will go through it all alone.

Though I have written a demand, one upheld by Rhineheld when I told him I would disinherit any child of Miracules with me, full stop, if he didn't aid me in my work to provide Avila comfort and to protect the life of my child with him. I think he didn't believe me at first, but I showed him that I have had lawyers draw up a second will which leaves no doubt as to my intentions, and I promised I would sign it should any harm come to Avila or our child at all.

Oh, yeah, did I mention? Miracules is pregnant. It seems my seed is strong and wolf-god makes a regular mockery of my prayers. But I also know wolf-god favors the determined man, and I will achieve my goals. Taking Rhineheld down a peg and Gregorus Rossi down entirely are now at the top of my list. Scorpius says he can control his older brother, the Rossi heir, and has him well in hand. We'll see. His side of things is still mystifying to me, and I can't tell if he wants to crown himself Lineage Leader, or simply be the brains behind his older brother's reign.

Whatever the case, I find my heart hardened to anyone who gets in the way of my plans to reunite with Avila. Including Miracules, though he is a kind person and even more beautiful when he's glowing with pregnancy. It only makes me angry to see him, though. Especially when I think of how Avila is probably not glowing right now. How he is unhappy.

I've read Avila's letter so many times and his final line guts me every time. How can I live a good and happy life when I know he's not being treated as the precious jewel he is? I told him so in the reply I entrusted to Scorpius. He promised he will deliver it unread and unaltered, and that he will help Avila either hide it or destroy it, so he isn't caught communicating with me.

In the letter I did tell him about Miracules and the other baby. I felt it was better he heard it from me, rather than some cruel whisper that might reach his ear. He is in isolation, but it is possible one of his cruel brothers might decide to sneak in to taunt him over it.

I hope the news doesn't hurt him too badly. But I know the opposite—him pregnant with another alpha's son—would gut me.

Still, I did it all for him.

Everything I do now is for him.

CHAPTER SIX

Year 659 of Wolf

AS THE SUN threatened to rise on the black horizon over the choppy sea, Vale skipped several more entries again. They were boring, if he recalled correctly, and all about the political machinations that Sian undertook in the course of being a better leader to his Lineage, and also to ferret out any potential leverage he could use to further provide Avila with a more comfortable life.

His main technique was to ask detailed questions about what people did around the estate, and within the Lineage. The more he asked, the more he learned, and before long it became clear to him who was valuable and who acted as more of a hanger-on, a dead weight to the Lineage as a whole. Those who didn't provide much to the family, or the estate, became uncomfortably aware of that fact as Sian questioned them. Desperate to hide their own uselessness, they all came to his side in any future argument.

It meant having dead weight hanging off the Lineage for some time, but if they were willing to cast their lot in with him, then Sian had been willing to put up with it. It made sense to Vale that Sian would take such a route during that time in his life.

With the dead weight's help, Sian had managed to pressure the Rossi family into giving Avila a comfortable bed, a rocking chair, fresh fruit, good meat, and time in the woods around the heat house he'd been confined to. It was all argued as being better for the health of the unborn child—which might be his heir—and with so much pressure from the Maxima elders and advisors (useless dead weight, almost all of them, according to Sian) the Rossi had given in.

Vale had enjoyed reading all the entries the first time around, and maybe he would enjoy reading them again since he would have access to the story whenever he wanted, but for now Vale skipped ahead to the next exciting bit.

He'd always loved this part of Sian and Avila's story, though it also broke his heart. If he felt a prickle of heat under his skin, he could ignore it for now. But only just for a little bit.

He had time. Not much, but...

There wasn't anything to be done about the

situation now either. He'd have to endure it whether he liked it or not.

With that in mind, he could distract himself with Sian and Avila's tale as he breathed through the initial warning waves of an oncoming heat. There were hours still before it hit fully.

Waking the household to ask for their help in containing him somewhere safe to suffer it alone could come later.

Sian Maxima's Journal
Year 137 of Wolf

JOURNAL, I SAW Avila and our son today.

Scorpius arrived three days ago to let me know our son had been delivered safely, and I immediately packed my bags, gathered a crew of Maxima men who now support me—amazing what useless sycophants will put on the line to cover up that they never have their actual ass on the line—and headed directly to the Rossi estate with Scorpius at my side.

At the gates I pitched the biggest fit in the history of fits until I was granted an audience with Gregorus Rossi. Then I demanded to see my son.

At first, they told me they would bring him to me, but I demanded to see where he was staying, in what conditions he was living in, and insisted I must see Avila too, since as my son's pater, his health determined the well-being of the babe.

There was some back and forth about that, but Scorpius took my side of things. Johann, the Rossi alpha heir, was ambivalent. In the end, it was Gregorus's favorite omega, Herry, the one whom he is married to, who tilted the table in my favor. He isn't Avila's pater, apparently, but he, like most omegas, has a softness for the travails of his sex.

He whispered in Gregorus's ear, and the man looked close to fainting at whatever words he said. I know they are not *Érosgápe*, so Herry cannot have the same sway over Gregorus as if he were, but favorite omegas still have great power. That is why everyone is so dead set against me being with Avila when they want me to be with others—or, as I have finally come to understand, they think they can control me by controlling access to him.

Well, they'll soon have quite the surprise coming their way, won't they?

In the end, Herry agreed to supervise my meeting with Avila and our son, along with Scorpius and a reluctant Johann. His father instructed him to go along, though it was clear he'd rather idle about the main house, doing whatever it is he does with his days as a spoiled heir. Probably the same as I used to do, frankly, before Scorpius and Dama helped me see I was squandering my power and my way to get Avila in my arms.

I did not get to hold him in my arms, journal.

But I did get to hold my son.

The heat house they moved him to is deep in the woods, but not a hut like those foul things they have up the mountain. The house is spare. Made of timber. With a few windows and a front porch where the rocking chair we arranged for him sits with a pleasant view of the valley below.

His kitchen is small but has a stove, table, and some cabinets, which seemed to hold a day or two's worth of food. There is a cold stream by the house, where he keeps the fruit and milk someone delivers to him every few days. It's not much, but it's not a nightmare.

Avila is weak though. His black hair is not as glossy as it was, his eyes have lost their shine, and the pallor of his skin worries me. Despite being a new pater, he is too thin.

My heart still beats only for him. I'm not so shallow as to have only loved him for his beauty, but it hurt to see him looking diminished and unwell. I wanted to tug him close and fight our way out of the Rossi estate together. But they'd taken my weapons before allowing me in the front gates to visit Gregorus, and Johann had a sword on him, even if he seemed too lethargic to use it. I didn't think we'd get past Valter, though, who'd also tagged along and stood on the front porch, refusing to even look at his *"ruined"* brother, but wanting to make sure I didn't get up to any *"dirty tricks."*

I loathe him. I will put a knife in his heart one day and not blink an eye over it.

Avila hadn't expected me. He was unkempt, alone with the babe, and his expression was all shock and then shame when I first walked in. That was the knife to *my* heart, journal. That he would look ashamed to see me.

I went to him, but before I could pull him into an embrace, Herry cleared his throat and Johann said, "None of that. You're here to see the baby, confirm his health. Nothing more."

Avila's eyes didn't meet mine as he held the squirming bundle of our flesh and blood out to me. I took him, because I didn't know what else to do, and Avila finally murmured, "He is healthy."

I asked, "But what about you, my love?"

He finally raised his gaze to mine, surprise and wonder there. "Me?"

I stepped close to him, not touching, but almost, and whispered, "I will save you, Avila. I will free you."

He glanced behind me at the others in the room and then looked down. "I'm doing well. They provide for me. It's more than I deserve."

I scoffed. "You deserve the world." I didn't care what they thought of my declaration. "You and this child will have everything and more. I promise you."

Avila met my eyes again, wet his dry lips, and whispered, "That's a lot to promise, Sian."

"Let's give them some privacy," Scorpius boomed. "He's not going to fuck him now. He's just given birth, for wolf-god's sake. Let them have a moment with their son."

"He doesn't deserve that," Valter snarled from the doorway. He wasn't looking in, but rather staring into the distance. "He doesn't get to have any happiness now."

"What bothers you more, brother? That Avila is loved, and you are not? Or that you can't take the love away from him no matter how hard you try?"

"I'm upholding the laws of our Lineage!"

"Why?"

"Because wolf-god values purity, and he's—"

"Are you so pure, brother? Haven't you been fucking that scrawny omega from the Chase Lineage? And you don't even love him, or he you, and yet you condemn Avila for loving the man he was with?"

"He didn't love him! He was in heat!"

"You dare to speak of heat?" Herry murmured, lacing his ring-clad fingers together and turning to glare at Valter. "Silence. Before I talk to your father about you."

"Yes, Pater," Valter said, grinding his jaw. "Forgive me, Pater."

"We'll wait on the front porch," Herry said. "With the door open."

Avila fairly swayed on his feet as the others left, and we were finally left alone except for the shifting, moving babe in my hands. Our son.

"Pull him close to your chest," Avila said, anxiously. "So you don't drop him."

I did as he asked, and the baby moved against me and then settled. Avila relaxed some. I reached for him, and he stepped away, his eyes darting to the door. "Avila," I whispered. "It's all right."

He reached out tentatively and touched my extended hand. His fingertips felt cold against my hot palm. He swayed again, and I grabbed him by the elbow, jostling the baby who mewled a little. Avila's dark brows furrowed, and he whispered, "I'm all right."

"Let's sit down," I said. "You've just given birth."

He nodded and let me lead him to the table. I

noticed immediately there were no comfortable chairs or a sofa for him, and I decided to make that right. The heat house was only one large room, not opulent and varied like the ones on our estate, and I wondered if the conditions were just a continuation of Avila's punishment, or if all heat houses on the Rossi estate were lacking in the finer amenities.

But my focus was mostly on Avila. I hadn't seen him in five months now, and he looked so changed. His cheekbones stood out. His dark lashes stayed down instead of lifting to show me glittering, amused glances like before.

"What's wrong?" I murmured, reaching out to stroke his cheek, but he pulled back. "Aside from all of this?" I let my hand fall to cradle the babe closer. He squirmed against me, as if looking for milk. "I swear to you, I'll free you as soon as—"

"You were with Miracules," he murmured. "He's due soon, I suppose? You should make a family with him. Marry him. You should be happy."

I frowned. "I was with him only for you."

He winced, shaking his head. "I asked you not to—"

"It was a deal I had to make. *That* for—" I motioned around at the house. "This. Rhineheld agreed to petition your father for these accommodations in exchange for…that."

Avila bit into his lip. "You spent the full heat with him?"

I shook my head. "I…" Clearing my throat, I felt a little frightened to admit the next part. Omegas didn't take well to alphas making light of the pain associated with an unrelieved heat. "I made him suffer until his father agreed to my stipulations. Until I could be assured of this house for you."

Avila shuddered and glanced up at me, his eyes a little wary. "My little alpha has some claws and teeth then?"

"Your little alpha will rip them all apart. Just give me a little time."

Avila darted a glance at the door and then reached out, shifting the blanket away from the baby's face, and said, "You haven't even looked at him."

I realized he was right. I'd been too busy gazing at Avila to do more than glance at the child we'd made.

He's beautiful, journal. Little black brows on his pale face, and lashes that touch his plump cheeks. His mouth is shaped like mine, but the rest of him is all Avila from what I can see. An angel. Like his pater.

"He's beautiful," I told him.

"He has all his fingers and toes," Avila said with

the first hint of his usual impish smile. "You can count them to be sure."

And I did count them. They were perfect and tiny. Little nails shining like slivers of almonds.

"That's enough," Valter said, coming into the room with Herry and Johann at his heels. "Sluts don't get the privilege of—"

Herry slapped his son, and the sound of it rang in the room. "Get out," he snapped. "Get out of my sight."

Valter rubbed his cheek and glared at his pater rebelliously enough that I passed the baby back to Avila and rose, ready to protect Herry from Valter if I must. I wasn't going to stand by and watch an omega be assaulted.

Valter turned on his heel and marched from the house. Johann patted the sword dangling at his side, as if he'd actually planned to use it—never! He's worthless, just as Scorpius has described.

"Let's go," Herry said, shaking out his hand and staring after his son. "He'll go talk to your father before I can, and it'll make things worse for everyone instead of better."

I didn't want to leave Avila. I wasn't sure when I would be able to see him again.

"My birthday is coming up," I told him. "I'll be at the age of majority."

"You'll be crowned Head of the Maxima Lineage," he said softly.

I nodded. "I'll have a lot more power. I won't have to answer to my council." I had to be careful not to say too much, not to alert Johann or Herry to the larger plans at hand. Scorpius and I will not be satisfied with simply getting Avila free. No, we will take them all down.

If I can't have Avila now, I'll have revenge.

Avila brought the baby up and kissed his cheek. I was envious. I wished he could kiss mine.

"Let's go," Johann said, motioning for me to leave. "He is in isolation. This was so you could see your son, not so you could rekindle your flame for him."

Herry shushed Johann, too, and the room fell silent for a moment.

"I'll see you and the baby again soon," I whispered, daring to reach out and stroke Avila's hair. It slipped through my fingers, and I wanted it back. I wanted to grip it and him and never let him out of my sight.

He nodded, kissing the baby's head again.

I was at the doorway already when I realized. I stopped and turned back around. Johann tried to grab my arm, but I shook him off. "What do you call him?"

Avila's lips turned up at the edges in a small smile. "Toivo. It means hope."

"Toivo Maxima," I said with a nod. "A good, strong name for an alpha."

"You don't know if he's an alpha," Johann said. "There's years to wait yet."

Of course he's right, I can't know for sure, only omegas can be determined at birth. But somehow, I just know.

"Toivo," I repeated, my eyes on Avila.

"Hope."

I stepped quickly across the room, grabbed Avila and the babe to me, and kissed his mouth once. Johann pulled me away. I swear, journal, when I finally grow taller—and surely I will grow again soon—I will never be physically torn from Avila again.

"Go on," Avila whispered. "We'll be here waiting."

I let Johann lead me to the door, swallowing hard, but my heart beat with encouragement. Avila hadn't given up on me, then. He believed me when I said I'd come for him, that I'd save him. And I will! As soon as I can!

Journal, I just need more time.

But wolf-god, how much time?

MIRACULES HAS DELIVERED our son. An omega.

So that's that. An end has come to Rhineheld's ambitions. I won't be pressured into mating with Miracules again. Soon, I'll wear the crown of this Lineage, and I've stopped letting myself be bowled over by the opinions of my former councilors.

As for Miracules's future, I've arranged for Scorpius to handle future heats with him. The connection between the Rossi and the Maxima Lineage will be further solidified that way. And Scorpius is a good man. He'll make a fine role model for my second son as he grows up, and I believe he'll treat Miracules well.

I certainly never loved Miracules, not even when I trembled on top of him through his heat. He deserves an alpha who will fall for his charms. As I've mentioned, he has many. Hopefully our son will inherit some of them. But, as of this morning when I went to the birthing rooms to meet him, the child looks like me.

It's a pity. His pater is truly a beautiful man.

Though not half as beautiful as Avila.

We're calling the baby Jela.

CHAPTER SEVEN

Year 659 of Wolf

"ARE YOU SURE?" Vale swallowed hard, sickness roiling in his gut. He stared at the doctor who'd helped him out of precarious situations in the past and felt himself grow light-headed.

The heat had come on harder and faster than he'd even known was possible. A rebound heat from his attempt to take dodgy heat suppressants had put off the timing of his cycle. His friends had tried to contain him, but he'd escaped.

He'd come out of the heat haze in a terrible part of town, covered in alphas' semen and his own slick, and aching all over from having been mounted by an unknown number of men.

The trauma of it had kept him from his work and poetry, had trapped him in humiliation, horror, and shame. The news that he was pregnant had been devastating. The highly illegal procedure to take care of that problem, undertaken in private, had been painful and emotional.

And now this?

"I'm sure."

It was unfair. Vale started laughing, a deep, hollow, horrible laugh that made the doctor lurch toward him in worry.

Fair? *Fair.* What a horrible concept to ever teach a child. Life was never fair.

Was it fair to Mr. Marks when the accident had taken away his ability to be a true alpha to an omega?

Was it fair to Jordy when his *Érosgápe* had been killed by a freak lightning strike two years after they'd found each other?

Was it fair to *Vale* when his parents had died, or he'd been left unclaimed, unwanted, and alone?

Fairness was absurd. If there was any lesson Mr. Marks should have told him to take from Sian's journal it should have been that life wasn't fair. Life was messy, and hard, and men struggled through it the best they could, living on cobbled-together hope.

Hope. Like Avila and Sian's Toivo.

He'd always wanted to have hope like that in his life. He'd dreamed of a child, of a new life to support and raise. But if what this doctor was telling him was right? He was well and truly hopeless.

That night, broken-hearted and alone, Vale snuggled deep into his bed and listened to the creaking of his empty house. His body ached, and he curled protectively around his middle, as his mind turned over the events that had led up to the horrible news he'd received today.

It was his fault. Blame, if there was any to be placed, could only be laid at his feet. He'd have to live with his choices and their consequences for the rest of his life.

At least there was no alpha to disappoint.

Restless and sad, Vale turned the light on beside his bed, and pulled out his copy of Sian's journal from the drawer in his bedside table. It was dog-eared now. Worn. He'd even violated the code of all booklovers and written notes and poems in the margins.

Tonight, he wanted to read the entries leading up to the climax of Sian's story.

If his life wasn't fair, at least it wasn't quite as miserable as Avila's had been.

Sian Maxima's Journal
Year 138 of Wolf

THE CORONATION IS over and done at last.

Three months ago, I turned twenty. Rhineheld delayed our official exchange of power as long as he could, insisting we wait until the end of the Autumn Nights Feasts in order to ensure wolf-god's blessing. The council agreed despite my protests.

The ceremony finally took place during the Feast of the Expectant Wolf, and now the Lineage is in my control.

I don't fool myself that I have everyone's loyalty yet. There are many who still defer to Rhineheld and expect me to do so as well. I overheard more than several comments about *"getting my feet wet"* and *"taking my time"* when it comes to taking full leadership.

But fuck that.

I have hardened my heart to anyone who stands in the way of me being with Avila.

AFTER THAT ANGRY entry, Sian's use of the journal was sparse for over a year. Intermittently, he ranted about the slow cruelty of time, the barbaric viciousness of Avila's family, the irritating calls for patience and prudence from Scorpius, but the overarching theme of it all was that Sian was denied access to his beloved at every turn. A visit to see his son was occasionally permitted, but only alone, not with Avila.

For Toivo's first and second birthdays, Sian traveled to see his son, and his journal entries from that time were full of both joy and despair. The boy grew well, he looked like Avila, and he seemed happy and was obviously well-loved by his pater. But it wasn't enough. How could it be enough?

Sian vowed revenge. He cried, and the ink was smudged with his tears.

Vale had little idea what the Rossi family gained from this brutality, aside from one Lineage leader's sadistic satisfaction at wielding power over another. Vale knew enough of the world now, though, to understand that pleasure taken in another's pain and suffering was more than enough reason. It was a common theme amongst men in power, as if the usual pleasures of life grew dull when too easily afforded.

Perhaps that was the trouble with wolf-god. He was all-powerful, wasn't he? Had he grown tired of the simple pleasures? Perhaps he was a sadist, too.

Vale put his blasphemous thoughts aside and read on, joining Sian on his path to reuniting, however briefly, with his Avila.

Sian Maxima's Journal
Year 139 of Wolf

RECENTLY, SOME OLDER men, old friends of my father's, expressed the opinion that my sour disposition is due to my foolhardy devotion to Avila. They said I would be happier without him, and encouraged me to be disloyal. They said I should have Toivo brought to me and move on with my life. "There are other handsome omegas," they said. "You should knot and breed them. It will clear your head."

"It's not as though you're *Érosgápe*," they said.

I'm not sure what they thought had changed since the last time advisors tried to convince me to turn my back on Avila. But just like those past advisors, these men are no longer welcome on the Maxima estate. They are free to see if they can beg a home amongst other Lineages, but they will never be allowed on Maxima land again.

I have no patience for old men who don't understand love or loyalty.

Speaking of Avila, I will be allowed to see him again soon—under the pretense of checking on my son, of course. I received news the baby was ill for a time, and I have insisted on a personal visit to verify his health *and* the conditions he's living in.

Not that my insistence means much to Gregorus

Rossi. But this time, if I'm not allowed to confirm my son's pater's well-being for myself, I have threatened to bring in wolf-god's own priests to audit Avila's case.

It's an empty threat of course. Most priests would be happy to see an omega punished for stepping out of line. On the other hand, setting an omega aside and naming him off-limits for breeding violates wolf-god's most important commandment: multiply and be fruitful.

Our numbers are not so great that priests won't see fit to insist on the Rossi breeding every fertile omega, no matter the omega's age, preference, or sin.

Truthfully, an audit from the priests could go either way for us. They may deem Avila's treatment fair, and we'd be no closer to gaining his freedom. Or they may declare that he *must* be made available to breed—and not necessarily by me.

It would be far too risky for me to go through with my threat, but I didn't need to.

At the mention of a potential audit by the priests, Gregorus capitulated. Failure to pass any part of their capricious investigations would result in disastrous consequences, not only in this world, but the next. Despite Gregorus's supposed-devotion to wolf-god's laws, he's terrified to face the priests' potential judgment. Most men are.

That's why Scorpius has been quietly bringing a few into our fold through blackmail. He uncovers a dark misdeed of theirs, or entraps them in one (usually sexual), at which point he has them by their not-so-pious balls.

I don't care how Scorpius procures their loyalty, so long as they don't hinder us in our plan.

Regardless, the good news is my petition was granted, and I leave in three days.

I both yearn to see Avila and yearn to murder the monsters who stand between us.

I must remain patient, though. Scorpius is still gathering soldiers on his side of things. We'll need more than just men of the Rossi and Maxima Lineages to pull this off. We'll need loyal volunteers from the Chase and Monhundy Lineages, too. At a minimum. Perhaps the Heelies as well.

In the end, the Council of Combined Lineages must acknowledge our claim.

What is that Old World saying? Heavy is the head that wears the crown?

Well, heavy is the heart that has everything but what it most wants.

I may be wealthy, crowned, and gaining power by the moment, but I still can't reach my Avila. I still can't bring him home.

It's been two years and three months since I saw Avila. Two years and three months since I pressed my lips to his. *Two years and three months.*

My rage grows alongside my grief.

And yet it still isn't "time," according to Scorpius. My patience is beyond frayed. Some days I think I will go feral from missing Avila and my inability to improve his lot. If not for Scorpius's guidance, I'd have acted by now.

And no doubt destroyed both of us in the process, leaving poor Toivo parentless. Not to mention leaving my Lineage leaderless.

So wait I must, and wait I do. My only recourse is to re-read the few letters Scorpius has been able to bring to me.

Two of the Seven Letters Sewn into Sian Maxima's Journal
Year 139 of Wolf

Dear Sian,

I am doing well. I think of you often and the summer days we spent together by the river. They were beautiful. I know you always thought I didn't believe you when you declared I would be yours one day, but the truth is I believed you instantly. There was such certainty in your voice and gaze. The way you crossed your arms over your chest and stated it like there was no other way for life to go…

I believed.

I still try to believe. It's been so long, though, and I admit my faith falters. I imagine you with your other son, your other omega—arrogant Miracules and his nice eyes—and I think ugly thoughts. But I'm better than that, or I believe you would want me to be, so I clear my mind of hateful thoughts as much as possible. I look at our son and think of how much like you he might be in spirit, if not in looks. He's stubborn like you. That's for sure.

He brings me joy every day.

Toivo is the light of my life.

You are the sun of my life. I wait for you to rise.

Your omega,
Avila

Dearest Sian,

Scorpius delivered your letter. I wish I didn't want your reassurances that I'm much more beautiful than Miracules, but I read them over a dozen times and tried very hard to believe you.

They've allowed me a mirror now and some nice brushes for my hair. Scorpius says they came from you, and that you blackmailed Johann into taking my part so I could have them. Something about an omega he dallied with but doesn't want to see punished? Could Johann be in love? These are questions I ponder as I brush my hair, empty hours stretching out ahead of me.

All of this just to say that I have seen myself. I'm not the man I was before. I feel quite sure Miracules is more handsome by far, but if your love for me blinds you to that fact, then I'll eagerly encourage it. I find myself quite jealous at the thought of you mating with him, handling his heat. And I'm envious beyond belief of the fact that you can spend part of every day with the child you share with him. Not that I begrudge you the joy. I want you to be happy. I want you to love Jela. You should!

I just wish Toivo had the same benefit of time with you.

Most fervently and selfishly of all, I wish

I did.

Scorpius tells me that Miracules is to be *his* omega from now on, and I have nothing to worry about.

Still, it's so quiet here, with only the birds and the squirrels and sometimes a falcon, and my mind plays tricks on me.

I begin to believe that I will never leave here. That they'll come to take Toivo from me, and I'll stay alone. That I won't see your face again.

I begin to fear that the day I came to see you, jittery with the oncoming heat and desperate to have you for myself, was the last I'll ever share with you like that.

And my memories of it aren't what I want them to be. Dirt floor. Both of us out of our minds. The pain of separation.

But the moments when you were knotted inside me were glorious.

And now there's Toivo. He's my joy.

I should be braver and send you stronger letters. I should tell you I'm fine, that I will survive it all. I shouldn't burden you or make you feel obligated to keep the promises you gave me as a boy, and again in the ecstasy of knotting and heat.

But I'm not that strong.

I know you love me. Deep down, I do.

And I do believe you'll come for me, Sian. In my heart.

But sometimes I'm scared, sometimes I'm so weak, and who else can I show my weakness to, if not you?

Forgive me for not being stronger and for not loving you more purely.

Your omega,
Avila

Sian Maxima's Journal
Year 139 of Wolf

JOURNAL, AVILA LOOKED terrible.

He clearly isn't eating well, and our child is skinny, too. Toivo is refusing to nurse since his sickness, and Avila is a jittery wreck about it. Not only for the health of our child, but if he's not nursing, that means Avila's heats will return soon. If a heat comes, not only must Avila suffer through it alone, but the child will be removed for the duration—perhaps longer. There's talk of sending the babe to me in that case.

I can't help but compare Toivo's smallness with

Jela's robust health.

It terrifies me to think Toivo could waste away, and I could lose both Avila and my son to these twisted, puritanical Rossi laws.

If they want to send Toivo to me, I think I will have to accept, for the sake of the child's life, but it undoes me to think of what it will do to Avila's sanity.

He's suffering mentally, even if he isn't being hurt physically. I've done all I can to relieve his doubts in my letters, but I can't send them as often as I'd like, since Scorpius is seen as too *"soft"* on his brother and has had his visits restricted.

Still, I did see him, if only briefly. I even got to hold him for a few precious seconds before Herry told Johann to break us apart. He was so small in my arms. I suppose I have grown after all. I'm now taller than he is, something I've always yearned to be, and yet it felt so wrong for him to slot in against me like he's wasting away.

But he still smells like heaven to me. Pure, perfect heaven.

He cried when I left. I won't forgive them for that.

I won't forgive them for any of this.

I HAD A meeting today with Scorpius, Dama, and a few other trusted men. We have a plan to deal with Avila's upcoming heat—the signs of which began to present two days ago according to Scorpius—but if it works in our favor, it'll unfortunately delay the execution of the final plan. We'll have to use up favors we'd intended to otherwise call in for the battle ahead.

Toivo is here with me at the Maxima estate now. Scorpius brought him to me when he came. He only shook his head when I asked how Avila took the removal of our son. That was all I needed to see for an arrow to stab my heart. If I can ever make this all up to Avila…

Wolf-god, I don't know how I possibly can, but I *will*.

I am consumed by if-onlys when I think of him lately:

If only I'd been stronger that day by the river.

If only I'd sent him away instead of pulling him closer.

If only I'd resisted my lustful need to be with him.

He'd be safe, and he'd be free, and maybe even here with me.

It's all too much for me to hold in my head and heart without wanting to throw our plan to the wolves and ride out to the Rossi estate on my own to attack at once, come what may. Scorpius and Dama have cooler heads. Which is for the best, I know, because all those if-onlys are nonsense.

What's done is done. We have a son. We must take this one step at a time.

Still, I hate that we took Toivo from him, even if the baby will do better here. My son will be given the best medical treatment to clear up his lingering cough. The best food. The warmest, safest rooms. I will love him and order that he is to be loved by all.

Miracules has agreed to care for Toivo and nurse him alongside Jela. He isn't bitter about the way things worked out between us. He's happy with Scorpius's attentions and looks forward to sharing his next heat with him.

Despite Scorpius having shared several heats with Rossi-approved omegas from other Lineages (virgins all, from what I understand) they were all barren. I've been told that often happens.

Not every man is as virile as I am, apparently, given that both times I've lain with an omega in heat my seed has taken hold. But Scorpius is a strong, healthy specimen, and Miracules is a fertile omega. No doubt they'll succeed when the time comes.

Rhineheld *is* bitter over my disinterest in Miracules. He holds a mighty grudge. But he can suck my dick. Because I hold a mighty grudge, too. Far stronger and crueler than his. If it weren't for the fact that he is my son's grandfather, I would probably murder him now instead of what I have planned for him. So, in that way, I suppose his plan to tie us together through the birth of a child worked after all.

Otherwise, I'd have slit his throat months ago.

When did I become so bloodthirsty, you may wonder? I'll tell you when.

When I left my beloved sobbing in a heap on the floor.

When I heard his cries echo through the valley as I rode away escorted by armed Rossi men.

When I remember that all of this, *all* of it, could have been avoided if they'd let me marry him when I wanted to, though I was still uncrowned.

When I remember it was Rhineheld's and the Rossi's political machinations and lust for power that damned my Avila to so much suffering and pain.

Now? I don't care who I must hurt, jail, or kill. I'll free Avila at any price.

But first, his heat.

Like I said, we have a plan…

JOURNAL, I COULD hear his screams from the valley as we worked our way up the muddy forest trail. It was raining, pitiless, ceaseless rain, and yet his cries carried. It was just me, Scorpius, Johann, and Dama, though there was a small regiment of men at the base of the hill and around the back of the house to prevent any attempt at me escaping with him.

As if I could have made it far with an omega in the throes of heat! Still, at least they know I am a real threat, and that I am serious about having him as my own one day.

At first, when I entered the cabin, soaked through, shivering, and covered with mud from a fall I'd taken over some exposed roots, he didn't seem to recognize me. His eyes were glazed with pain as he writhed naked on the floor. He was covered with slick. The overwhelming scent of his need had permeated the room.

I shut the door behind me, blocking out Scorpius, Dama, and Johann, and barred it from the inside with a chair from the kitchen. I had swallowed some of the alpha quell on the way up so I would be able to control my desire, and I took a moment to check the kitchen—it was not well-stocked, but it would be enough to get us through the heat.

Then I called out for them to leave us.

My voice seemed to rouse Avila from his agony,

and he turned his head to me, eyes focusing for a moment. Then he was gone again, and I quickly stripped, eager to relieve him of his pain and suffering.

The first knot was on the floor. Just like the first time we were together, but at least this floor was wood and not packed dirt.

The second knot, though, was in his bed, and it smelled so deliciously of him I didn't last long at all.

The third knot... Well, that one took a bit longer, and I was able to give him the kind of pleasure he has always deserved from the start. I took my time, kissing him, loving him, adoring him, until he begged me to knot him, and when I did, he gazed up at me with such clarity in his eyes as he whispered, "I love you, Sian. I am made for you."

We are not *Érosgápe*, but I believe him.

We made love endlessly, for days and days as the heat demanded, and it was everything I could have wished for, and yet nothing about it was right at all. Because we are still unmarried. He is still locked away from me. I was escorted out of his house after the heat ended by armed men. He is still considered ruined by his family.

They'll regret it in the end.

But I cannot regret being there with him. It felt right to be in his arms, to be servicing his needs, and to take my pleasure in him as well. I yearn to have him with me now, safe in my home, safe in my bed. I'll feed him every delicious thing imaginable, I'll pamper him with the best perfumes, the softest clothes, the finest pillows, and he'll never hurt or suffer or want for anything ever again. I'll pleasure him daily. I'll love him always.

I'll kill them all.

AVILA IS PREGNANT.

What can I say? My seed is just that strong.

But I won't wait another day. I can't allow him to go through another birth alone.

I've summoned Scorpius. It's now or never.

They had their chance to be reasonable. Now they will suffer the consequences.

CHAPTER EIGHT

Year 660 of Wolf

"SUFFER THE CONSEQUENCES," Vale read aloud, putting the journal aside and staring at the flames as they sank lower into the grate.

"What a gruesome idiom," his new alpha friend Urho said, swirling his liquor in the short, cut crystal glass Vale had filled for him earlier. They were at Urho's country house, between waves of a receding heat, reading aloud to each other from books they each liked. Vale had chosen Sian and Avila's story.

"Why must we always suffer the consequences? Why can't we dance in them?" Urho asked.

Vale tore his gaze from the fire and looked at the man next to him in the bed. It had been a good romp. A fun week. They'd already agreed to spend his next heat together. But it wasn't love.

Still, Vale liked the way Urho thought. "Dance in the consequences, huh?"

"Sure," Urho said and stood. His lean, tall body

was muscled, and covered with smooth, umber-colored skin and a dusting of black hair. He was beautiful, and suffering consequences, too, having lost his *Érosgápe* in childbirth a few years earlier. "Let's dance."

"There's no music," Vale protested, but let himself be pulled into his friend's arms.

"I'll hum."

The heat of the room dissolved into the prickling beneath his skin, another wave rising slowly as they swayed and held each other. Vale tilted his head back, his cock hardening, his hole going wet with slick, and he moaned. Urho grew hard against him, too, his powerful alpha cock throbbing against Vale's thighs.

They rutted together, passion growing, until Vale found himself tossed onto the bed again, Urho's hand on his throat as he fucked into him hard and long, and finally, *finally* knotted him.

Blanking out with an orgasm that swallowed him whole, Vale trembled and shook, lost in pleasure as the heat took him hard. "*This,*" he gritted out. "I deserve this."

Dancing in the consequences, free of suffering.

"I *deserve* this."

Urho hummed his agreement.

Heat was like violence, consuming and driven,

and Vale surrendered to it without reservation. Taking what was his by design and by right. If pleasure was his gift, it was also his punishment, and he'd grab it with both hands. With all his rage. All his hurt. All his need.

Greedily.

Sian Maxima's Journal
Year 139 of Wolf

IT FELT GOOD to hold Rhineheld's throat in my hands and squeeze until his eyes bulged. I might have gone further except for Miracules's screams. I suppose the handsome omega with the fine eyes *does* have some sway over me emotionally after all; he takes good care of both of my children.

Instead of killing Rhineheld, I ordered him arrested, and now he sits in a jail cell writing endless screeds about how I'm too young to rule, how I'm unstable, how I'm obsessed. Perhaps so, especially the part about me being obsessed. I'm obsessed with Avila and have been since I was a child. He should have paid more attention to that instead of pushing for his own ambitions.

Well, he *was* writing screeds that is. Up until I threatened to kill Emeldo, Rhineheld's omega, if he didn't stop bad-mouthing me. He shut the fuck up pretty wolf-god quick after that. Amazing how alphas get so attached to their omegas, even non-*Érosgápe* ones. Funny how that attachment can be used to control them, to hurt them. He seriously didn't think I wouldn't have learned that much from him? Or that I wouldn't use his tricks against him? He assumed incorrectly that I didn't have the cutthroat instinct to get what I want as well.

He held Avila over my head to get his way, and now I will hold his precious Emeldo over his to get mine.

However, just between you and me, I wouldn't have actually killed Emeldo. Again, Miracules's tears over his pater would have bothered me far too much in the end. (Wolf-god damn the connection!) But it's an effective threat to keep Rhineheld in line. For a time.

Now the Maxima estate is entirely under my control. Rhineheld and his cronies are dealt with. The people kneel for me and do what they can to please me in every way, offering things I don't even want—sex being chief amongst them, frankly. I always decline these physical offerings, but I do accept some of the other gifts and gestures of obeisance. This scraping and bowing from them is not my preference, truly. I never imagined myself the type to wear my crown outside official business, for example, but I find it a good reminder to them of who's in charge now, and so wear it everywhere. Until they see me as the legitimate and only power in the Maxima Lineage, keeping my people guessing as to what will please me is necessary.

Next up...

We're going to get my omega and bring him home.

Which leads me to the Rossi portion of the plan. Scorpius should already be laying the nets. Now we must snap them closed. Won't they all be so surprised? Won't it feel good to have Avila in my arms?

If the people of my Lineage fear me now, they'll fear me even more when word gets back to them of what I'll do to any Rossi who gets in my way. I'll bring Avila home with me, no matter what the cost. My people will not protest the connection. I'll see to that with the power I'll gain through this small coup. My leadership will be strong enough to stamp out any rebellion or any attempt to reinstall Rhineheld in a position of authority ever again.

No, I never wanted to lead by fear...

But nothing else has worked: diplomacy, compromise, outright begging.

So fear it is.

CHAPTER NINE

Year 660 of Wolf

VALE RELISHED THIS part of the tale. He pondered it as he sipped whiskey in his pater's old library, the printed journal open on his lap and the roaring fire licking at the grate deliriously.

The puritanical, devout-as-fuck Rossi had never seen it coming. They'd never thought for a moment that a non-*Érosgápe* coupling could generate a love so intense it would overpower the strictures against murder, as laid out in the Holy Book of Wolf.

Érosgápe mates? Certainly. There was no stopping the pull of that bond. That was why *Érosgápe* were granted every exception known. It was a dangerous connection in every way.

But other loves? Not nearly so strong. And the population was still so small, the need for more children from every possible alpha and omega so high, and the work of the betas so necessary to a functioning society, it hadn't entered their minds at all that Sian and Scorpius might kill for what they wanted.

And yet kill they had.

Vale remembered from his upper-level history research into Avila and Sian's lives how the Maxima Lineage had arrived at the Rossi gates with a full regiment of armed men, as well as reinforcements from the Chase and Monhundy Lineages. They'd refused to take no for an answer when the guards had denied them entry. Those guards had been the first to die, at the points of arrows fired from the rear of the small army.

Within the Rossi estate itself, chaos had already erupted. Scorpius had rallied his supporters, made up of lower-ranked alphas, many betas, and even some omegas who were tired of being treated so harshly, and they'd taken Scorpius's brothers hostage and wrestled his father into a jail cell.

Scorpius had waited then, patient as a simmering pot, until Sian arrived with his reinforcements. Then the trial had begun.

If it could be called that.

Sian sat on the Rossi throne at the top of the stairs leading to the front door of the main house with Scorpius standing at his side. One by one they'd dragged the leaders of the Rossi Lineage out before him, and between Scorpius's growling questions, and Sian's shouted ones, they narrowed down who was to live and who was to die.

Those granted a reprieve had groveled on their knees, making promises of loyalty and fealty, before they'd even fully understood what had happened. It wasn't until Gregorus Rossi was brought to Sian, hands tied behind his back and eyes wide with shock, that the gathered people of the Lineage, surrounded by Maxima, Chase, Monhundy men and the supporters of Scorpius, truly understood what was happening.

Vale knew Sian had left most of the questioning of Gregorus to Scorpius, for he had many grievances against his father, as did the people of the Rossi in general. Before long, the crowd was on their side, as Scorpius trotted out every violation, every hypocrisy, every cruelty, every denial, every agony that Gregorus had visited on his Lineage.

But history books claimed Sian Maxima asked Gregorus only one question: *Did you deny me marriage to Avila Rossi?*

Sian hadn't waited for Gregorus to answer before drawing his knife and cutting Gregorus's throat. Sian then took the offered crown from Scorpius, placed it on his own head, and declared himself the Lineage Leader of both Maxima and Rossi, combining the Lineages into one, and claiming the land between the estates as well.

It was brutal. It was quick. And it was over.

Time distorted many things, but it was clear that no one ever dared to question Sian or Scorpius again. They kept their power throughout their lives, and their children kept it through theirs.

The Maxima were, even now, some of the wealthiest and most powerful people in wolf-god's new world.

Vale's pater had almost contracted with one until he'd met Vale's father and their *Érosgápe* bond was revealed. He'd never seemed to regret the loss of wealth, not when he'd had the bond of that great love.

Vale sipped his whiskey again, listening to the fire roaring in the otherwise eerily silent house. The logs collapsed, sending up sparks.

Perhaps he should get a cat.

Turning back to the journal, he read on…

Sian Maxima's Journal
Year 139 of Wolf

AVILA IS SAFE.

Though I think he's a little afraid of me now. I swept into his heat house at night, covered in his father's blood and wearing his father's crown, followed by dozens of men bearing candles and singing a song of holy praise to me. Blasphemous, really, and I knew it then, but I didn't care.

All I cared about was Avila.

I found him hiding behind his bed, crouched over his swelling stomach, protecting it, protecting our child from whatever was coming their way. He didn't know of our plan. He didn't know it was me barging in the door. He cowered, and I think he is ashamed of that.

But I'm not. He was without a weapon. He is with child. Our child.

I have him now, and he's safe.

He's *safe*.

I took him into my arms, and he shook against me. I kissed him and he allowed it, but he didn't kiss me back. He stared at me like I was a vision— not necessarily a welcome one. As if I were a man he couldn't recognize.

When I saw myself in the mirror beside his bed, ablaze in the candlelight, I admit I barely recognized myself. I was stained in blood and wide-eyed with battle lust. I'd never killed before—I hope to never do it again—but it had powered me like a stallion in a storm, racing hard against the weather, racing against the rain, the thunder, and trampling whatever was in my way.

Relentless.

I must have scared him. Still, he let me hold him close as we took the path down the mountain. He was so exhausted by the time we reached the bottom that I had to order a horse to take him all the way to the main house. There he was bowled over by his omega brothers who all greeted him with a mingling of tears, cheers, and tales of the horror I'd wrought.

As if he couldn't see the blood there on the steps leading up to the house with his own eyes.

Again, Avila turned and looked at me as if I were a stranger. It chilled me and sent my heart tumbling.

But I am the same man I've always been. I'm no less stubborn. I *will* show him I'm still his Sian, and he is still my Avila. Nothing can change that.

I may have to woo him, calm him, but I will make him see I'm still the Sian he loved by the riverside as a boy.

Just a little older.

Just a little bloodier.

IT'S BEEN TWO days since the slaughter. That's what they're calling it, and I'm fine with that description. We did kill a good number of Rossi men. I should feel more guilty about it, but I don't. They took my omega from me and kept him. They made me mate with another. They stuffed me through endless political and social hoops. They forced him to suffer. They put us through hell.

That fucker Valter had laughed at our pain.

Well, he wasn't laughing when Scorpius's man cut his throat.

Neither was Johann when we gave him the choice between death and life in prison. He took the latter because he's useless but not a fool.

As for Herry, I hated to do it, but Scorpius and I both knew he was going to be a problem. I banished him from the Maxima estate, and he's been taken in by the Sabel Lineage. They'll treat him well—better than he deserves. Though I suppose it wasn't his fault what happened to my Avila, and at times he did try to ease things for us, but at other times he used our situation to his own political advantage, too.

No, Herry was *not* going to stay on any estate ruled over by my Lineage.

I want to take Avila home immediately, to reunite him with Toivo, but Scorpius and Dama warn against it. Both of them insist I must stay here on the former Rossi estate in order to fully establish my authority and reign over the Lineage. They say any other choice will allow rumors to foment and lies to spread. What we did was heinous enough; we don't need to allow any further degradation of the truth. We killed men, but we aren't going to make life harder for the living.

Soon they'll see. We'll make things *better* for them here. Then they'll be glad of our strength. We got rid of all the men who benefited from the old way of things. Now all who remain stand to do nothing but gain: privileges, wealth, new houses, happier omegas.

Betas stand to gain better wages. Omegas will have a better life, full stop.

Already there is a sense of relief amongst the omegas. I had the heat huts razed yesterday, and I've declared no heat will go unmatched from now on— unless that is an omega's choice. The Rossi omegas seemed shocked into silence or tears at the announcement. Though there were protests from a few devout omegas who continue to believe their pain during any unmarried heat is wolf-god's just punishment for the past impurity of their souls, I informed them that while they can suffer if they like, their beliefs cannot be forced on others. The majority are happy to be matched. I've received a flood of food and drink and flowers delivered with effusive gratitude over the last day.

I've given them all to Avila.

Speaking of, Avila is housed in the Lineage Leader's rooms here—once his father's and Herry's, now his. I can see it makes him uncomfortable. *I* also make him uncomfortable now. He flinches away from me, as though he can still see the blood on me. I must find a way to get through to him. I did this for him. For us.

But in the end, it will benefit so many more. That's what Scorpius helped me to see. That's what took so long. We had to get everything into place to ensure we could help as many people as possible. I'll be a better leader than Gregorus Rossi, and Scorpius will be my second. He plans to marry Miracules, and I will marry Avila, and then our houses will be joined completely.

But first, I must convince Avila I haven't turned into a monster.

A Letter Sewn into Sian Maxima's Journal
Year 139 of Wolf

Dear Sian,

Of course I don't think you're a monster. I just don't know how to understand the way my life has changed so suddenly, or to accept you were the agent of that change in such a bloody and murderous fashion.

It's not as if I loved my father—not anymore—but I respected him and his laws. I believed for most of my youth that he knew what wolf-god wanted, and I honored his position on those things.

I even believed I deserved to be locked away after tempting you into our first encounter.

I hated being punished, but I understood it. This new world, this new you...

I don't understand these things.

I'm glad you wrote to me, though you are only sitting across the room by the fire pretending like you aren't watching me out of the corner of your eye. I see you. But this way I can write to you as well. It's easier to say this all on paper than to look you in the face and say it aloud.

Your eyes aren't like they used to be. They're darker now.

You're darker now.

But I am, still, your omega,
Avila

Sian's Reply Sewn into Sian Maxima's Journal
Year 139 of Wolf

My Beloved,

You are different now, too, slimmer, haunted, and shorter than me. Remember how I used to come up to your chin? Remember how when you first let me kiss you, you had to duck your head and I had to go onto my toes?

Some of those differences, like my height, were bound to happen in the natural course of things. Others, like your frailty, were brought about by others' actions. The pain you've suffered... It makes me come unhinged to think about it too much.

Is that an excuse I use for what I did?

Yes. It is my excuse. Wolf-god alone can judge me for it.

I'm not ashamed to have taken the satisfaction I did in ending your father's life, but I suppose I should have washed his blood off before rushing to you. I wanted to make sure you were secure. You're my weakness. If there was one part of the plan that could have gone wrong, it was that someone might have gotten to you before I could; they could have hurt you or worse.

So I came to you immediately, and I frightened you. I understand. And perhaps my eyes are different now. They've seen so much. I've watched useless men grovel, I've watched powerful men abuse, and I've watched my own hand run a blade through a man's throat.

I've also seen our child getting healthier by the day, looking more like you, looking so handsome with your big black eyes and dark brows. I've seen other Lineages and how they treat omegas—so different from how the Rossi do—and I've seen how brutal your father was to his own sons, especially to you. I know now what a man will make another man do for power. I've done some of those things.

And yes. I killed for you, for us, and for a future that will be different for all omegas of your Lineage.

Becoming a man who can kill has changed me.

We must accept I'm not the little boy by the river anymore because I'm no longer innocent or naïve. But I am a man who will love you until the end of time. I am the man who plotted and schemed and did things he hated in order for you (and all the omegas of your Lineage) to be safe. I am the man who loves you. I'm your son's father—and your unborn son's father—and I am your alpha.

Forgive me for being weak that night by the river. Forgive me for following you to that awful hut instead of sending you back to your bed. Forgive me for knotting you. Forgive me for the pain you suffered. Forgive me for everything because it's all been my fault. I had to make it right for you in any way I could.

Forgive me for killing your father, and your brothers, and forgive me for taking so long to do it.

Forgive me.

You're all I need and without your forgiveness it's all been for nothing.

Your alpha,
Sian

WRITING LETTERS BACK and forth was a good idea, journal, and I'm glad I proposed it. Sometimes I'm smarter than people give me credit for, though I do still rely on Dama and Scorpius for input on a lot of my political decisions. This, however, was wholly my idea, and Avila didn't hold back in writing, the way he had been whenever I tried to talk to him face-to-face.

In the end, after reading my letter, he came to sit by me on the bed and touched my cheeks. He kissed my mouth, but not passionately, as if he were testing the softness of my lips. I was tempted to reach out for him, but I didn't want to scare him more than I already had, so I sat very still and let him decide how to proceed.

In the end, he pulled me down next to him, and we lay on our sides just breathing and looking at each other.

Eventually he fell asleep. This was progress, though. He's been alone for so long now, and this is all so sudden from his point of view. I've been working on this coup for ages now, but I never gave him any details. It was too risky to write them down even here in these pages. I'd been saying for years I was going to get Avila at whatever cost, but no one took me seriously, and so long as no one except my co-conspirators had any details of our plan I knew it would remain that way.

So this—the sudden release from his prison, the loss of his father and many of his brothers, the change in me—has all been quite the shock to him. He deserves time to adjust. I've waited patiently (well, maybe not that patiently) for so long I am quite all right with waiting a little longer for him to grow comfortable with me once more. Being able to see him, to know he is never going to suffer alone again is all I need.

His swollen belly grows daily, and the new child will be due before we know it. I make sure he has the best food for every meal, and I can already see some health returning to his cheeks. Now I just want to see the brightness return to his eyes.

Miracules is bringing Toivo tomorrow. That will surely bring a smile to Avila's pale face. Seeing his son will invigorate him, no doubt.

CHAPTER TEN

Sian Maxima's Journal
Year 139 of Wolf

I SHOULD HAVE seen the tension between Miracules and Avila coming, but I admit I did not. I'm a foolish alpha, I suppose, but I've never thought much about Miracules aside from him being Jela's pater, and so I didn't anticipate the way Avila might react to his presence, or at seeing him with Toivo.

The day started out nicely with the two of us sharing breakfast. There was some color in Avila's cheeks, excitement in his bearing, since he knew his son would arrive soon. He kept asking me if he looked all right, asking if I thought Toivo would remember him—though it's only been a few months since Toivo was brought to live with me.

The sun was high when the carriage arrived with Miracules and the children. I was greeted by both of them running over on their toddler legs, both smiling wide and throwing themselves on me. Jela looks far too much like me. Poor boy, he should have at least had Miracules's fine eyes. When I picked them both up, carrying them toward Avila…

Well, perhaps that was my mistake. I should have only picked up Toivo and left Jela for Miracules to handle. But it isn't the boy's fault I'm his father! That he looks like me! It *isn't* the boy's fault. Whatever was going on in Avila's heart, he will have to accept that Jela, like Toivo, loves me.

I turned to Avila, smiling, and said, "Look at our family."

Dama later told me that was my second mistake.

Avila's jaw tightened as he took in Jela, and then he swooped in and grabbed Toivo from me, kissing his cheeks fervently. The baby clung to him, crying out, "Pah-der!" in his sweet, lisping way, and Avila shot Miracules a look as dark as any I've ever seen from him. Avila whirled away—his long black hair slapping my face—and took Toivo into the main house without a backward glance.

Miracules met my eyes and shrugged. "He's always been a jealous sort. He used to glare at me whenever I mentioned you and my father's plans for us, even back when we were all just boys."

That was news to me, journal. I had no idea I'd ever been a topic of conversation with the omegas of the various Lineages aside from the things Avila had told me—that they thought I was cute and would make a good alpha one day—but apparently, according to Miracules, I was much discussed, and Avila had hated it.

"He once told me in a snit that my nice eyes wouldn't be enough for you," Miracules said, taking hold of Scorpius's arm as the three of us went up the stairs together. "And he was right, wasn't he? You never wanted me. I don't know what he's so angry about."

But I knew.

Avila had come to the riverside that night long ago because he hadn't wanted me to be with Miracules. He'd begged me to refuse. Then he'd been punished for wanting and having me, while Miracules had gotten what Avila had never wished him to have—a heat with me, and now a son. Because of that Miracules now lived a life of privilege and care, all while Avila had suffered alone.

It's a mess, journal, but what can I do about it? What's done is done. I wouldn't trade Jela for the world. I love him. Miracules is nothing to me aside from Jela's pater. But how do I make Avila understand?

I can love both my sons.

I'd like for Avila to love them both too.

But perhaps that's too much to ask?

143

AVILA IS SO happy to have Toivo with him, and the babe is thrilled to be with his pater, too. Avila is nursing him again, which seems to be good for them both. They are such a happy pair. They wander the fields together, and Toivo is learning the fun of pulling petals from the wildflowers they find there, and Avila is rediscovering the joy of tucking flowers into his dark hair. He looks like a jewel when he returns from these walks—eyes glossy, hair filled with petals, and a softness to his smile that I've missed.

We talked about Miracules last night. It was necessary.

Avila has refused to take dinner at the same table as the man he sees as his rival. It's absurd. I wouldn't have slit anyone's throat for Miracules! (Though I suppose I *didn't* slit one throat in particular for him—Rhineheld lives, after all—and that's more than I will ever tell Avila!)

Last night, though, I went to Avila's rooms— previously Gregorus and Herry's. Toivo was asleep in the middle of his big bed, and I sat in the ornate chair beside it. Avila was tense at first, sensing some sort of confrontation or demand from me, but as I spoke, he eased more and more.

"Miracules is no one to me."

"I know."

"Do you?"

He shrugged, his long lashes touching his cheekbones again, hiding his eyes.

"Avila, my love, he's Jela's pater—"

"I know that too," he growled.

"And?"

Avila wouldn't meet my gaze, turning his attention to where Toivo's chubby thighs were spread wide. He ran a finger over them, and Toivo blew a bubble in his sleep.

"Do you think I love Jela more than Toivo?" I asked.

Avila's shoulders slumped.

"Ridiculous."

"He looks like you," Avila said before touching his bulging, shifting stomach. "Maybe this one will look like you too, and you'll love him like you love Jela."

I laughed. "Beloved, listen to me. Toivo looks like *you*. The man I adore more than anything in the world. The man I killed for. The man I've shaped my world around." I leaned closer to him, and he didn't move away. "Toivo is far more beautiful to me than Jela, if you must know."

"Is he?"

I nodded, scooting from the chair to the bed so I could admire my son. "He has your eyes, and eyebrows, and the way he smiles—" I clutched my chest. "It takes my breath away how much he looks like you then."

"When it was just Toivo and me in the heat house," Avila began carefully, feathering his fingers through our son's black tufts of hair. "I wished he looked like you every day. I wanted proof of you."

"Proof of me?"

"Yes, sometimes everything about my old life started to feel like a dream. I even doubted you'd ever existed, or that you loved me and would come for me. With Toivo there, I was less lonely, I had him to focus on, but he looked nothing like you, and so I worried..." He let out a slow breath that made my heart hurt. "I worried I had lost my mind. Made you up. Maybe it was just me and Toivo all alone in the world."

"Would you make up an arrogant little shit who declared you to be *his* the very first time he met you?" I asked, keeping my eyes on Toivo's chest as it expanded with his breath. "Surely not."

"You've always been my dream alpha," Avila confessed. "Even when you showed up covered in my father's blood to carry me out..." He squeezed his eyes closed, and I dared to take hold of his hand.

He didn't pull away. "Do you know how often I dreamed of just that? I was so angry some days, Sian. I wanted them all dead. Part of me fears I made it happen with my rage. That I killed my father."

"Your father killed himself," I gritted out. "My hand might have held the blade, but he cut his own throat. He had chances—so many chances—to do the right thing by you and the other omegas here."

"But he didn't believe it was the right thing," Avila whispered. "He was a true believer. A devout worshiper of wolf-god."

"Devoutly wrong."

"Yes, but…" Avila tugged his hand away, and I felt sure, journal, I had ruined the moment. "Some people love the wrong way. They can't help it. Maybe I have loved the wrong way."

"When?"

"When I'm jealous of another man and his son with you." Avila's lips twitched up at the corner. "When I want to spit in his face. When I want to poke out his nice eyes."

I reached for his hand again. "What nice eyes? You've always said that about him, but I don't think they compare at all to yours."

Avila laughed and said, "You're not a good liar."

"I'd take looking into your eyes over looking into his any day."

Avila's breath hitched. "*That* I believe."

"I do love Jela," I said quietly. "He's my son. I wish you could find it in your heart to forgive him for being born."

Avila's cheeks grew pink, and he pushed his long hair behind his ears, looking up at the ceiling as if calling up strength. "I'll find a way. It's not his fault you and his pater... That it happened."

"You know I did it for you."

Avila's face twisted but then he nodded. "I remember."

I took a deep breath, journal, and did something that could have backfired spectacularly, but I couldn't resist. I reached out and slipped my hands into his hair, running my fingers down to the ends, and tugging lightly. He leaned toward me, his eyes on my mouth, and this time when I kissed him, he gripped me close, and the kiss quickly turned passionate.

I believe it would have escalated, but Toivo woke, and his cry broke us apart.

Avila's mouth was swollen from our kisses as he drew the boy into his arms and opened his tunic to expose his nipple—already dripping with milk for our unborn babe and Toivo—and our son latched on.

I cuddled both of them close, smelling Avila's

fragrant hair, and watching as our son fed until his eyes drooped, and he fell asleep again.

The moment was perfect.

Soon enough the new baby will come, and we will be an even more complete family.

JOURNAL, I'M FILLED with joy for the first time in what feels like a lifetime.

Avila came to me last night, well past the last bells, and climbed into my bed. I woke, confused at first, but then I scented his perfection and drew him close. He was already aroused and ready for me—his prick hard and his hole wet with slick. I was shocked at how quickly he urged me into him. The swelling of our child inside his thin frame made it necessary to take him on his side, but he kept one of my hands pressed to his mouth, kissing my fingers the whole time.

The pressure and heat, the slickness, the scent of him, the sounds he made! The way he came around me and spurted his pleasure all over my sheets! The way he urged me on, and on, and on, until I lost my load deep inside him, pulsing with my orgasm and biting his exposed shoulder lightly to keep in a scream.

Journal, these descriptions may sound crass, but it was glorious. The closest to heaven I've ever been. Heat has its beauty, but this non-heat-fueled coupling is so much more precious to me for being entirely voluntary, entirely Avila's idea, and purely for pleasure and to express our love.

He clung to me afterward, slept in my arms, and when he woke leaking milk for Toivo, he bid me to bring the boy to him. So I fetched him from Avila's rooms and watched him feed our son in the moonlight, still covered in my scent.

I believe we are going to heal from all this pain.

Avila is going to be all right. He will be mine, and we will finally be happy.

YOU KNOW WHAT they say, journal, about one step forward and two steps back?

I don't think Avila has taken two steps back from me today, but he is being distant again. He didn't come to my rooms last night, and I didn't want to push him by going to his. If he needs space to feel things about what we did together, I will give it to him.

I'm a very patient (impatient) man.

I can wait for him to come to me again.

AVILA RETURNED TO me last night, demanding to
know why it was I hadn't come to him the night
before. He was fiery about it, let me tell you! His
eyes were bright like they were when we were
younger, but with anger, and he hissed the question
at me as he shed his clothes like someone had dared
him to do it.

"I wasn't sure you'd want me," I murmured,
pulling back my bedclothes to let him in.

"Of course I want you," he snapped. "That's
why I came to you first. Don't make me beg for it,
Sian. Don't make me feel like that."

I wasn't sure what he meant, but I've heard from
Scorpius and Dama both that omegas are mysterious
beings, so I agreed and promised not to make him
beg, or at least not to make him wait for me ever
again. (Begging in bed is another matter!) I'll go to
his room every night if that's what he wants.

Last night he wanted me for hours, and I gave
him every drop of my seed and every ounce of my
love. He was exhausted and shaking by the time I
finished with him. Luckily, Toivo slept through the
night. I don't think Avila would have had anything
left to give him, for I drank from him deeply myself
as we made love.

A beta servant brought Toivo to us this morning. Our small son looked wide-eyed and afraid, but his arms stretched out for his pater as soon as he saw him. "Pah-der, hold me."

Avila comforted him with kisses to both cheeks and the sweetest of hugs. I watched, delighted by the vision of them propped up on a dozen of my pillows, dreamily rumpled and happy in my bed.

A perfect morning.

Worth every sacrifice.

CHAPTER ELEVEN

Year 661 of Wolf

VALE LEFT THE empty, quiet house behind and headed out into the autumn air. The leaves were piling up on the sidewalk leading from the house to the gate, and he supposed he should do something about that.

But they were pretty as they were, like gold and yellow stars piled on top of each other in a shimmering heap. He bent to pick one up, twirling the bright yellow leaf by the stem as he walked on.

He pondered the journal he'd left off reading the night before. He'd always loved Avila's jealousy of Miracules. He thought he'd be jealous in the same situation too, even if it wasn't fair.

There were times he feared he'd somehow find his *Érosgápe* only to discover he was already contracted to another omega and had several children with him. But all the wishful thinking about *Érosgápe*s was fading away. He was getting too old. The time had passed. And if he did find one, there was no doubt it'd be exactly that: he'd be the interloper in a family. The most beloved interloper, yes, but still a mess.

Vale was done dreaming of children, too. Paterhood was a train he'd derailed and would never again get the opportunity to ride. It bothered him to feel stripped so decisively of a future he'd once thought was inevitable, but there was nothing he could do about it.

Now, after months of considering it, he was getting a cat.

Because a cat, his own house, and a career writing poetry would make up for everything else he didn't have. It *had* to…

Wolf-god help him if it didn't.

The pet shop was empty of people when Vale went inside, and the beta owner gave him a quick nod before continuing to stock jars of pet food.

The back wall of the shop was lined with crates and cages, and Vale passed by the puppies and rodent-like pets. At the end of the row was a crate with a litter of kittens rolling around on top of each other. He peered inside and counted six. Three black, two a kind of blue-gray, and one almost silver. The gleaming fur caught his eye, and he reached inside to pull it free.

"That 'un's a girl," the shopkeep said, having

come over to see if he could help.

"A *girl*." The concept of females was still amazing to Vale, though he'd long known it was only the human females who'd been affected by the Great Death.

The kitten peered up at him, meowed, and then bit his finger harder than he expected.

"I'll take her."

"She's a pretty one."

As he worked his wallet from his pocket, the silver kitten jumped free of his arms and darted through the store.

"Oh, wolf-god, these kittens are quick as the wind," the shopkeeper said, taking Vale's money, then coming around to help him chase the kitten around the store.

"Wind is right," Vale said, when he'd caught her and held her head tight under his chin, feeling her purrs. "I think I'll call her Zephyr. A soft wind."

On the way home, carrying Zephyr in the little carrier he'd bought for her, he listened to her plaintive meows and cooed soothing sounds to her in response.

He'd make dinner, wear her out with play, and then read by the fire again tonight. Perhaps it wasn't the life he'd dreamed of, but it was the life he intended to make.

He was no Old World king or Lineage Leader from the early years of Wolf, and he didn't have a love that set his heart ablaze, but he had a home, a kitten, and good whiskey. He had poetry and a life of his choosing. Many omegas would kill for the freedom he enjoyed.

Vale should remember that.

Sian Maxima's Journal
Year 139 of Wolf

TODAY MY AVILA was crowned beside me. We were married in front of wolf-god and all the people of our Lineages.

After all that has happened for us to come to this zenith, I'd expected it to feel much more momentous. But it was simple, really, more of an announcement of what had always been true: my heart is Avila's for life, and his is mine, we are alpha and omega, the beginning and end forever.

We exchanged promises and vows.

Our son stood next to us on his wobbly legs.

Avila accepted the crown of my Lineage, and I wear the crown of his.

The priest announced our covenant and proclaimed us Lineage Leader and Leader's Omega of the combined Maxima and Rossi lines and declared both would be known as Maxima from now on. I'd asked Avila if he preferred to use a hyphen, or combine our names, but he said he didn't want his father's legacy to live on. Since his father had tortured Avila more than me, I didn't question his choice.

Afterward, during the celebrations, I called for the attention of our people and announced new laws for omegas. Never again will omegas of our Lineage go unmatched for their heats. Never again will omegas be given to an alpha without their consent. I'd consulted Avila on the other new laws, too, and I'd also talked with Miracules (with Avila present) to pick his brain for the best practices from our Lineage, as well as what could be improved back home as well. I still must work within the framework provided by the priests, lest we go afoul of wolf-god's actual law or stir up antipathy against our Lineage, but overall the omegas' situations will be much improved.

I'm already on the priests' watch list. I did, after all, kill men. That is decidedly against wolf-god's law. But, as I'd long suspected, the priests had always resented the way the Rossi prevented their omegas from optimal reproduction. So while I'm being more lenient with our omegas' sex lives than many priests would like, they also think more children will be born under these new regulations than under the prior Rossi rules.

But this doesn't change that I'm known as the Slaughterer amongst the other Lineages, and the fear is evident in their eyes. Scorpius is my second-in-command, and he's known as the Traitor. It's got to be a bitter pill for him, but he swallows it down without complaint. He has power, he has Miracules, he has someone to blame if things go wrong—me— and his older brothers are out of his way.

If it weren't for Jela, I might worry Scorpius would turn on me one day, too, but we'll share a son once he's married to Miracules, and that's a tie that's hard to break. Rhineheld was right about that. Besides, Scorpius likes to make tough decisions behind the scenes and let me take the fall for them; he also has very little need for credit or glory. He leaves those to me, like he leaves me the blame.

We make a good team.

Avila and I make a good team, too. As he's opened up to me again, I've shared my political problems and decisions with him, and he's given me welcome advice. Often his views are similar to Dama's or Scorpius's, but he typically offers up a unique perspective as well. He has an omega's point of view, and his insight into how my choices affect the men of my Lineage who suffer heats and bear our sons is helpful and important to me.

Avila also likes to be of use. He and Miracules have become—well, not friendly, but perhaps teammates in their desire to keep the estates running well. Scorpius and Miracules will take over the Rossi estate and Avila, Toivo, and I are moving back to the Maxima estate before the baby comes.

That could be any day.

I look forward to showing Avila the beauty of my home. The palace, the woods, the path down to the sea, and the waves that crash on the shore. But most of all, I want him to have the best care through the birth. If I lost him now, after all we've been through...

But I can't think of it.

Three days from now we will leave for my home. I'll continue to lead the Lineage from there, and Scorpius will run the estate here. I'll visit often. As I said, we make a good team.

I used to believe omegas existed to lift alphas up, if only to be deserving of the love of our omega mates, but now I believe it goes both ways. Alphas exist to lift omegas up, to treasure them, and make their lives as beautiful as possible. It's the only way forward in this dark world—honoring our omega mates, loving them without reservation or conditions. If our omega mates aren't safe and happy, then our world isn't safe and happy. That's the lesson I've come to understand.

That's the understanding I wish to impart to my people.

160

CHAPTER TWELVE

Year 661 of Wolf

THERE WERE ONLY a few more entries in the journal, including a short one announcing the birth of their second child:

We have another healthy son! An omega! We are calling him Cayo! It means joy. Avila is healthy and strong. That's all that matters to me. This—our family—is all that matters in all the world to me.

After that, there was a big jump in time before the next entry, which was about some political shenanigans Sian was dealing with, and then the entries tapered off until they finally stopped altogether. Vale thought perhaps with Avila by his side, Sian no longer had any need to share his heart with a page, not when he could share it with his man.

Vale regretted he would never know what Avila thought of the Maxima estate, or what little Toivo thought of his new brother once he came. There was so much of Sian and Avila's lives that would always remain a mystery. History told him that the Maxima went on to be one of the most progressive Lineages in the treatment of omegas and omega rights, but that didn't give any insight into their hearts.

One thing Vale appreciated, though, was that the appendices of the printed journal included a previously unseen note written by Avila recording a specific moment in his life with Sian. Based on the ages of their sons, it must have been at least fifteen years later…

Note of Avila Maxima

TODAY MY SIAN and I were in the forest of the old Rossi portion of our estate walking, listening to the birds, and enjoying one another's company. Ahead by the banks of the riverbed where I first met Sian, we heard the distinctive sound of our first-born's shout, followed by strong words yelled in anger. We rushed toward the sound of his voice, but then we halted just out of sight, seeing Toivo standing on the bank with Jela and an alpha named Bright.

"I will kill you," Toivo growled, taking a step forward.

Jela moved between his brother and the alpha he's been seeing, and Bright grabbed his sleeve to tug him back.

"I swear to wolf-god," Toivo said, pacing forward, his expression deadly dark. "You're dead."

Sian nearly leapt into the middle of things, as he is wont to do, but I held him back and whispered for him to wait. I wanted to understand what was happening before we broke into the disagreement. Jela and Toivo often fight, and quite dramatically, but they usually make up on their own. As for Bright's involvement… Well, I thought it would be a good opportunity to see how he handled conflict in case things with Jela grow more serious.

"Get your hands off my brother," Toivo gritted out, tugging Bright's fingers from Jela's sleeve.

"Stop," Jela said, softly, but Toivo didn't listen.

"If you've hurt him, I swear I'll not only kill you, but I'll make you *suffer* first."

Bright put his hands in the air and backed away from both of our boys. "I would never hurt Jela. I'm courting him."

"Courting him?" Toivo spat on the ground. "He'd never have *you*. He has better taste than that."

"What's wrong with *me*?" Bright bristled, and Jela's cheeks grew red as he looked at the ground and said nothing.

"Well, you're…you're…" Toivo trailed off, his gaze swinging back to Jela. He studied his brother and then scoffed. "Is it *true*? You like him?"

Jela nodded.

Toivo threw his hands up. "*Why?* He's an ass! He used to push Sanders around, and—"

"I've apologized to Sanders," Bright said, seriously. "And to his parents for the insult to their son."

Toivo snorted. "You didn't apologize to me for the insult to my best friend."

Bright bowed his head. "Allow me—"

"On your knees," Toivo said imperiously. "Like all good apologies should be made."

"Toivo, for wolf-god's sake," Jela exclaimed, tossing his hands into the air just like his brother had and much like their father does. "Bright's going to handle my upcoming heat. Father said it was all right. My pater and Scorpius approve. Leave him alone."

Toivo gaped for a moment, his gaze shifting between Jela and Bright. Finally, stepping closer to Jela, he examined his expression. "Truly? You like this little bastard? Don't you know he's nothing but a huge ball of horny alpha hormones? And he's kind of dumb about it too?"

"Hey!" Bright said from where he was kneeling on the ground by Toivo's feet ready to make the unfairly demanded apology.

"I do," Jela said, lifting his chin. "I know all that."

Toivo sighed, shook his head, and then sighed again. "All right," he said softly, patting Jela's cheek. "All right then." He turned to Bright. "Get up. I mean, my brother clearly has no taste at all, but if you're what he wants, then I support him."

Bright rose carefully. "I promise I'll—"

"You better," Toivo growled again before Bright could even finish. "Because if I hear of even one little—"

"Toivo," Jela said, taking hold of his brother's arm again. "He gets it. You're the big bad alpha on this estate, and you're going to inherit the Lineage, and he better be good to me or else."

"He better."

"He will," Bright pledged. "I mean, I will."

Toivo sighed. "I'd like it so much more if you would take Sanders instead."

"Well, I don't want Sanders."

Toivo seemed to accept that and then put out his hand to Bright. "Fine. Please forgive me for being an ass, though I'm still sorry my brother likes you."

"On your knees," Jela said quite cheekily, and I almost laughed, which would have given us away, hidden as we were in the trees. "Like any good apology should be given."

"Don't push it," Toivo said, kissing his brother's forehead, and then glaring warningly at Bright again. "Fine then. Whatever. I'm off."

"Hunting?" Jela asked.

Toivo shook his head, a small shy smile coming over his face. "Headed up to the old house in the hills."

"Ohhhh, is Trinity waiting for you there?"

"Maybe."

"Did you ask Trinity's parents if you could have him?"

Toivo scoffed. "Of course."

Then he set off up the hill to the house he'd been born in, and where I spent three long years of misery. It heals my heart knowing it's been reclaimed by lovers meeting up for stolen moments, even if it seems impossible that one of those lovers is my first-born son.

"Toivo doesn't like him," Sian said thoughtfully, staring hard at Bright through the trees. "Scorpius does, though, and Miracules says he has very good manners. Jela likes him very much. But if Toivo doesn't, perhaps I need to reconsider—"

"No. Toivo is just worried for Jela."

"What about this bullying of Sanders?"

"Bright only pushed Sanders around because Sanders pushed him around first. It was just two alphas flexing. Typical adolescent silliness. Toivo has a soft spot for Sanders, that's all."

"Yes, they've been friends a long time. Maybe he'd be better for Jela."

"Jela just said he doesn't want him."

"True. But does it need to be Bright?"

"Jela has chosen him, and Toivo will get used to it. Come, it's been resolved well enough without our help," I said, tugging his sleeve, and leading him further up the hill, past the old, overgrown path that had once led to the wretched heat huts. Sian left his worries behind and followed me easily when I used one of our codes for *make love to me in the woods*: "Didn't you say there's a blackberry bush that's come into fruit?"

He did indeed find a blackberry bush that was in fruit: me.

I wished to record all this for several reasons:

First, because I'm grateful for the brotherly love between Jela and Toivo. I know they will protect and care for each other for years to come. Our other sons will all do well on their own, but Jela has always needed Toivo, and, in his own way, Toivo has always needed Jela. They were born so close together and raised almost as twins. They are each other's mirror images, and I have relinquished any regret or poisonous envy I once held about Jela's existence.

Second, because our life is wonderful, Sian's and

mine. We struggle as all couples do, and though Sian has troubles as all leaders will, we are happy, and our sons are strong. They are, all four of them, perhaps too-stubborn men who know what they want. But I believe they will always do the right thing for themselves and for others.

With wolf-god's grace, I trust the Lineage is in good hands.

I know I always am with my Sian.

Year 661 of Wolf

HAVING PUT THE journal aside and corralled the tumble-happy kitten into a large box for a nap, Vale stretched out on the leather sofa in the library with a pad of paper and a finely sharpened pencil. He considered his life: the small tragedies and victories of it.

No one would write his story. No history books would bear his name.

He might never have an *Érosgápe*, or even an alpha of his own to love with all his heart, but that was in part his own choice. He wouldn't settle, like his old librarian Mr. Marks had, for simple companionship as a guard against loneliness. That was what friends were for, as well as a certain friendly alpha who had agreed to handle his heats from now on.

No, if he were ever to truly join his life with an alpha's in a contract, the man would have to be someone amazing. Someone beyond his wildest dreams. Maybe someone like that *was* still out there... After all, Vale was young and life was long. He might still be loved.

Vale scratched out the beginning of a poem:

If I suffer as Avila suffered
Then I must be loved as Avila was loved
I will never accept less

THE END

Vale collides with his destiny in SLOW HEAT!
Buy or read it now!

Letter from Leta

Dear Reader,

Thank you so much for reading *White Heat*, the prequel to the *Heat of Love* series! If you enjoyed this book, look out for the passionate and emotionally complex story of Vale and Jason in *SLOW HEAT*.

Extra stories for *Heat of Love* and other book universes can be found by joining my newsletter.

Be sure to follow me on BookBub to be notified of new releases in this series and others. And look for me on Facebook for snippets of the day-to-day writing life. I'm also on Instagram, so add me there, too!

If you enjoyed the book, please take a moment to leave a review! Reviews not only help readers determine if a book is for them, but also help a book show up in searches.

Also, for the audiobook connoisseur, the first all currently published books in the series, *Slow Heat*, *Alpha Heat*, *Bitter Heat*, and *Slow Birth* are available at most retailers that sell audio. They're narrated by the talented Michael Ferraiuolo.

Thank you for being a reader!
Leta

Book 1 in the Heat of Love series

SLOW HEAT

by Leta Blake

A lustful young alpha meets his match in an older omega with a past.

Professor Vale Aman has crafted a good life for himself. An unbonded omega in his mid-thirties, he's long since given up hope that he'll meet a compatible alpha, let alone his destined mate. He's fulfilled by his career, his poetry, his cat, and his friends.

When Jason Sabel, a much younger alpha, imprints on Vale in a shocking and public way, longings are ignited that can't be ignored. Fighting their strong sexual urges, Jason and Vale must agree to contract with each other before they can consummate their passion.

But for Vale, being with Jason means giving up his independence and placing his future in the hands of an untested alpha—as well as facing the scars of his own tumultuous past. He isn't sure it's worth it. But Jason isn't giving up his destined mate without a fight.

Book 2 in the Heat of Love series

ALPHA HEAT

by Leta Blake

A desperate young alpha. An older alpha with a hero complex. A forbidden love that can't be denied.

Young Xan Heelies knows he can never have what he truly wants: a passionate romance and happy-ever-after with another alpha. It's not only forbidden by the prevailing faith of the land, but such acts are illegal.

Urho Chase is a middle-aged alpha with a heart-breaking past. Careful, controlled, and steadfast, his friends dub him old-fashioned and staid. When Urho discovers a dangerous side to Xan's life that he never imagined, his world is rocked and he's consumed by desire. The carefully sewn seams that held him together after the loss of his omega and son come apart—and so does he.

But to love each other and make a life together, Xan and Urho risk utter ruin. With the acceptance and support of Caleb, Xan's asexual and aromantic omega and dear friend, they must find the strength to embrace danger and build the family they deserve.

Book 2.5 in the Heat of Love series

SLOW BIRTH

by Leta Blake

Jason and Vale are back in this side story set in the *Heat of Love* universe!

A romantic getaway turns dramatic when an unexpected heat descends on Vale, leaving Jason with no choice but to act. The resulting pregnancy is dangerous for Vale and terrifying for Jason, but with the help of friends and family, they choose to embrace their uncertain future. Together they find all the love, joy, and heat they need to guide them through!

While this story follows the characters from *Slow Heat*, it would be most enjoyable if read directly after *Alpha Heat*, as it takes place contemporaneously with that book.

Book 3 in the Heat of Love series

BITTER HEAT
by Leta Blake

A pregnant omega trapped in a desperate situation. An unattached alpha with a lot to prove. And an unexpected fall into love that could save them both.

Kerry Monkburn is contracted to a violent alpha in prison for brutal crimes. Now pregnant with the alpha's child, he lives high in the mountains, far above the city that once lured him in with promises of a better life. Enduring bitterness and fear, Kerry flirts with putting an end to his life of darkness, but fate intervenes.

Janus Heelies has made mistakes in the past. In an effort to redeem himself, integrity has become the watchword for his future. Training as a nurse under the only doctor willing to take him on, Janus is resolute in his intentions: he will live cleanly in the mountains and avoid all inappropriate affairs. But he doesn't anticipate the pull that Kerry exercises on his heart and mind.

As the question of Kerry's future health and safety comes to an explosive head, only the intervention of fate will see these desperate men through to a happy ending.

Leta Blake's latest Omegaverse novel

BULLY FOR SALE

Heat can be sold but love is earned.

In a world where heats can be sold for profit, Ezer has seen firsthand the cruelties of the world. He knows what's expected from his kind—timid compliance and submission to his "betters." But Ezer isn't one to roll over and conform to the role society has forced upon him.

Despite his defiant nature, Ezer is coerced into partnering with a man of his father's choosing. One his father promises will love and care for him for the rest of his life.

A night of nameless and faceless passion later, Ezer is horrified to find himself bound to Ned, a bully who has done so much to make his life hell. Ezer's determined to hate Ned but he can't help the way his body craves his touch.

Ned is young, privileged, and hopelessly in love with Ezer. Too bad his pack of so-called "friends" have targeted Ezer for torment. Ned has a lot of regrets, but none greater than his role in Ezer's misery. When Ned's offered the contract of a lifetime, he sees it as the only way forward with the man he loves.

The dual biological drives of heat and its aftermath might be all that's keeping them close now, but Ned is determined to prove he's worthy of Ezer's love.

While Ezer is just as determined not to fall for his bully.

Bully for Sale is a standalone m/m romance set in the *Heat for Sale* universe featuring forced proximity, first times, bully romance, opposites attract, and enemies to lovers. Content warnings will be available at start of book, visible via the Look Inside and sample.

Another Omegaverse novel by Leta Blake

HEAT FOR SALE

Heat can be sold but love is earned.

In a world where omegas sell their heats for profit, Adrien is a university student in need of funding. With no family to fall back on, he reluctantly allows the university's matcher to offer his virgin heat for auction online. Anxious, but aware this is the reality of life for all omegas, Adrien hopes whoever wins his heat will be kind.

Heath—a wealthy, older alpha—is rocked by the young man's resemblance to his dead lover, Nathan. When Heath discovers Adrien is Nathan's lost son from his first heat years before they met, he becomes obsessed with the idea of reclaiming a piece of Nathan.

Heath buys Adrien's heat with only one motivation: to impregnate Adrien, claim the child, and move on. But their undeniable passion shocks him. Adrien doesn't know what to make of the handsome, mysterious stranger he's pledged his body to, but he's soon swept away in the heat of the moment and surrenders to Heath entirely.

Once Adrien is pregnant, Heath secrets him away to his immense and secluded home. As the birth draws near, Heath grows to love Adrien for the man he is, not just for his connection to Nathan. Unaware of Heath's past with his omega parent and coming to depend on him heart and soul, Adrien begins to fall as well.

But as their love blossoms, Nathan's shadow looms. Can Heath keep his new love and the child they've made together once Adrien discovers his secrets?

Heat for Sale is a stand-alone m/m erotic romance by Leta Blake. Infused with a du Maurier *Rebecca*-style secret, it features a well-realized omegaverse, an age-gap, dominance and submission, heats, knotting, and scorching hot scenes.

Gay Romance Newsletter

Leta's newsletter will keep you up to date on her latest releases, sales and deals, future writing plans, and more from the world of M/M romance. Join Leta's mailing list today.

Other Books by Leta Blake

Contemporary

Will & Patrick Wake Up Married
Will & Patrick's Endless Honeymoon
Cowboy Seeks Husband
The Difference Between
Bring on Forever
Stay Lucky

Sports

The River Leith

The Training Season Series
Training Season
Training Complex

Musicians

Smoky Mountain Dreams
Vespertine

New Adult

Punching the V-Card

'90s Coming of Age Series
Pictures of You
You Are Not Me

Winter Holidays

North's Pole

The Mr. Christmas Series
Mr. Frosty Pants
Mr. Naughty List
Mr. Jingle Bells

A Boy for All Seasons
My December Daddy

Fantasy

Any Given Lifetime

Re-imagined Fairy Tales

Flight
Levity

Paranormal & Shifters

Angel Undone
Omega Mine

Horror

Raise Up Heart

Omegaverse

Heat of Love Series
Slow Heat
Alpha Heat
Slow Birth
Bitter Heat

For Sale Series
Heat for Sale
Bully for Sale

Audiobooks
letablake.com/audiobooks

Discover more about the author online

Leta Blake
letablake.com

About the Author

Author of the bestselling book *Smoky Mountain Dreams* and fan favorites like *Training Season*, *Will & Patrick Wake Up Married*, and *Slow Heat*, Leta Blake has been captivating M/M Romance readers for over a decade. Whether writing contemporary romance or fantasy, she puts her psychology background to use creating complex characters and love stories that feel real. At home in the Southern U.S., Leta works hard at achieving balance between her writing and her family life.

Made in the USA
Columbia, SC
13 February 2023

11859322R00119